Harrow's Gate

By

Lawrence BoarerPitchford

Second Edition 2019

Copyright © 2016 Lawrence BoarerPitchford

ISBN 10: 0-9896629-4-2
ISBN-13: 987-0-9896629-4-9

DEDICATION

Thanks to my wife, family, and friends for all your support and faith in my ability to spin yarns. Also, much appreciation goes out to my fans, for whom without their support, I'd have little impetus to keep telling stories.

A special thanks to my sister for her editing eye and support of my art! Thanks sis!!

CONTENTS

ACKNOWLEDGMENTS

NOTICE
The situations, characters, and concepts in this novel are the sole invention of the author.

Credits:

Cover Artist ~ Lawrence BoarerPitchford

Senior Editor ~ Wendy Schirmer

AUGERLAND

Prologue

A blue planet circles a yellow star. Once, upon its face, arrived several races, but not all at once. The last to arrive and settle were descendants of creatures that once dwelt in trees, many light years away.

They came and founded a civilization and prospered. They grew a culture and bathed in the light of technology. A utopia, one might say, rose up and flourished. That is, until they destroyed themselves – as all advanced races do.

In the aftermath, some of those destructive creatures managed to find refuge upon a continent they named Augerland. From there, the culture split, and split again, creating new colonies – governments – and traditions. Yet, the nature of those creatures called human will not fail to ruin, and strive forth to murder and lay ruin at the doorstep of their brethren.

~Excerpt from The Tome of Vergil Height

Chapter 1

A light in a darkened room illuminated a large tabletop map. The island of Burkmuran was in the upper left, and the small island of Palitz was just below it. The continent of Augerland was to the right with its known geographic features of lakes and valleys painted on the surface.

Other features like mountains and cities were made from wooden blocks. Cities were identified with colored pins topped with white strips of paper that contained the name of each.

Gunter Ault, the Supreme Dictator of Burkmuran, stood facing the map. His narrow nose and severe eyes were fixed firmly on the Augerland landmass.

"Let's get started," Gunter began. He turned and pointed with a long thin dowel at the northern island of Palitz. "We will stage the navy here at the southern point of Palitz."

He directed the pointer to the continent. "Our ships will position here, here, and here. The area between these two points of land is close enough for our navy to seal the Hurgray ships in their harbor.

"We will soften their coastal defenses with a navel bombardment launched from twelve dreadnoughts." Gunter pointed at a dozen models of naval ships in a semicircle positioned just outside the harbor of the city of Tiquan. He adjusted the pointer and tapped several tin airships hanging over the bay.

"From the air, our airships will have

excellent targets. Drop five hundred pound payloads here, here, and here." He pointed at the shipyards, steam-wheel station, and the airship landing zones.

"The Hurgrians have their navy anchored closely together which will make our sky attack very effective. Once their ships are neutralized, we can land our troops here," he pointed north along the coast, "and here," he pointed south.

"I don't have to tell you how important it is to our goals to secure the Hurgray capital and these beachheads. Once we've taken that continental port, our ships will blockade the inlet, and our troops will secure the city."

The Supreme Dictator turned to Kistler Vet, his Group General who stood next to him. He nodded then spoke.

"Group General, you will secure the southern borders and the east access to the desert at Harrow's Gate."

Gunter looked at his officers. "Subdue any attempt at counter attack, and crush any resistance. Group General."

Kistler nodded back, cleared his throat, and began. "The Hurgrian army has bases scattered across Hurgray, but they are mostly ill-trained militia forces, all volunteers. They will be easily swept aside by our gun-rollers and shock troops. Use the rollers to crush any resistance, and then have the infantry clean up those still opposing us. Round up any prisoners and ship them back to Tiquan. We'll use their own prisons to detain political and military malcontents."

Kistler adjusted his dark blue visor-hat.

"The only issue currently left unspoken is the overland trade routes to and from the Phol Empire in the south." He pointed at the map. "Use maximum force with the settlers along the desert side of the eastern Killiman Mountains. They're free-landers and known for their unconformity."

Gunter surveyed the darkness of the room as if he were looking out upon an audience.

"We've also had a stroke of luck. Our agents in Hurgray tell us that both men who command the largest shipping companies on the continent will be in Tiquan. The Niva family, and the Garland family will make good hostages, as we intend to abduct their children to hold as collateral."

Gunter reached down along the edge of the map and picked up a glass of water. He drank down the contents and then resumed.

"Franz Niva will be reticent to do anything that would jeopardize his only son's life. The Garland family has two children; a boy and a girl. I am sure that Mr. Garland will be loath to see them dead, so he and his company will be impotent at helping the Hurgrians." He turned to a guard at the far door. " Let in Major Foltz."

A man in a smart tweed jacket and black trousers entered and approached the table. He stopped and saluted.

"Special agent Heinz Foltz reporting as ordered."

Gunter saluted, and then motioned for Heinz to stand at the table, then turned back to the darkness to speak.

"Once we have the children, they will be

swept onto a dreadnought and held until our victory is complete. Without resupply of food and ammunition, the Hurgrians will be forced to surrender." Gunter turned to Foltz. "Now, where will we find our young guests?"

Foltz pointed at the map. "Emerald Garland will be in Tiquan from the tenth to the fifteenth of next month to inspect his new warehouses. His family will be traveling with him, and staying at the Green Bow Hotel near the middle of the city. Franz Niva will be secretly visiting his friend Lord Bowland at West Pincer Abby House during the same time." He indicated a blue pin inland on the continent. "Also, Franz's son, Leland Niva, will be arriving onboard the Valliant - one of his father's fastest cargo ships. "We are very sure he will venture into the city, for he's a twenty two-year-old youth."

"How soon will our agents in Hurgray secure the children?" Gunter asked.

"They are making preparations to intercept them as we speak, Supreme Dictator," Foltz said. "Once our invading forces have secured the city, Mr. Niva and Mr. Garland will be picked up by the Suspol and also imprisoned."

"We attack Hurgray in eleven days." Gunter said as he turned to Kistler. "Group General, ensure that the airships have all that they need. Have six of our Dreadnaughts begin interdiction in the south."

Gunter waved his hand, and the lights came up. Half a dozen junior officers were in the room sitting at desks.

"You all know what to do. Soon the

resources of the continent will be ours for the taking, and Burkmuran will become the greatest empire that has ever been."

***

The blade was snug just below Leland's Adam's apple. Sweat beaded up on his forehead. One false move and his life would be forfeit.

Don't be stupid, he told himself, *be cool*.

For many years he'd been warned, and on this day he chose to ignore the danger.

No matter, he thought, *there's a time in a man's life when he has to take action*!

Up along his neck the blade glided. The sound reminded him of rough sandpaper on hard wood. In the mirror, looking back, was his sudsy face; Leland Niva, son of the shipping tycoon Franz Oliver Niva.

He washed the blade and placed it against a foamy area on his neck and drew it upward. Again the sandpaper sound filled his ears. This was his first time shaving himself; a small task for most young men, but not for Leland.

At fifteen his father had insisted on letting the barber always do the work, even to the protest of his son. It seemed unfair, since all his friends were allowed to shave themselves.

"You're my only son," his father said. "I'll be damned if I'm going to let you cut your own throat and leave our family without an heir!" The man was serious, and not to be disobeyed.

So it came as a complete surprise when his father suggested that he accompany Carter Wayne to Tiquan. Leland jumped at the chance. He'd known Carter Wayne his whole life, for he was his father's second-in-command, and the father of his best friend, Tommy Wayne.

A long standing friendship had developed over the years, stretching from Leland's days in the nursery, to when he and Tommy graduated from the Kepler Boarding School. This was his chance; once away from his home, and out to sea, he'd finally taste some independence, even if it was under the supervision of his father's *right-hand* man.

Finally, at twenty two, he was sent to learn how the shipping business worked. Also, it would be his moment in the sun to learn about the world; after all, he did not want to forever be dependent on others.

Leland smiled. It was an absurd thought, to have a barber always shave him. He knew it was a sign of manhood to shave, and he would not be denied that rite of passage.

A bang at the door startled him, and he frowned as he set down the razor and put his finger over a bloody nick on his neck.

"What is it?"

"Lee, how much longer you going to be?" Tommy asked, his voice bombarding him through the door. "It's like waiting for a Pearl Town fancy lass."

"You almost caused me to cut my own throat, you ass!"

"You should let me do it, I'd probably do a better job," Tommy said.

"Mottel yer mom," Leland said back.

Laughter echoed from behind the door;

Leland turned back to his task. He reached to the side of the mirror and took hold of a brass wheel that controlled the shape of the surface. He cranked it until his image was enlarged.

Leaning into the mirror, his image became ultra-magnified.

"Yuck," Leland said, as his pores came into clear focus.

He examined the tiny wound, then applied some antiseptic-stick to it. It burned like hell, but he showed no expression of pain.

Quickly readjusting the mirror, he finished his task. He washed off the excess soap, then gazed at his image… piercing blue eyes, narrow nose, brooding brow… a younger image of his father.

Grabbing the white towel from the rod, he dried his face and exited the washroom. Tommy was sitting on the small red couch near the hatch.

"Thought you were grubben yer nub in there." He chuckled.

"Mottel yer mom," Leland said again.

"Charming," Tommy stated. "Would you kiss your governess with that mouth?"

Leland smirked. "I would."

"Tommy, Leland, get on deck!" the stout voice of Carter Wayne roared from the passageway.

Leland nodded to Tommy, then shouted back, "Aye, immediately, Mister Wayne."

Both men exited into the hall. The passageway to the main deck-door wound through the ship, marked by a painted yellow line. Brass banisters led upward along a set of black iron steps. As Tommy and Leland reached the top, a blast of cool, damp, brackish air washed over them.

Carter stood at the railing gazing out towards the city. "Come take a look," he said.

A set of four massive statues came into view. Each was built on its own small island; the four small islands that marked the path into Tiquan Harbor.

White seabirds circled overhead squawking and chawing. Carter leaned on the wooden rail.

"Take a gander at that. The Four Masters of Tiquan," Carter said. "They never fail to impress."

Leland stood in stunned silence. They were truly massive; each more than two hundred feet tall. He'd never seen such a thing, except as images in school books, but now here they were. One was standing holding a book. Another was pointing toward the city docks, and the third held a lantern that pulsed with light. The last had its arms wide as if embracing all who came forth.

"Hard to believe that they're just thin copper skins shaped over iron framed skeletons," said Carter.

"Look at the scripts," Tommy shouted as they passed the first statue.

Letters ten feet tall ran along the base of the monument's pedestal.

"Let thee read the scriptures and gather the hopes of man," Tommy read aloud.

"I want to take a tour as soon as we land," Leland said.

Carter chuckled. "There's work to do first. Your father didn't send you with me to sightsee - first work, then liberty."

Leland smiled. "You're the boss," he said. "I guess I should learn the business if I'm going to one day own it."

Carter nodded. "Quite mature for such a young man, Master Leland." He pointed toward a vast array of berths already filled with ships. "Look there! Guardian Star ships offloading cargo."

Leland shook his head. "How is it that they get the best berths?"

Carter put his arm around Leland's shoulder. "They got here first. First come, first serve – in Tiquan bay. I don't like those bastards either, but those new ships are faster - faster than the Valliant even."

"Not for long," Leland said.

"Ya, I can't wait for the new G class ships to roll out of the yards. That'll make the Garland family green with envy," Tommy said.

"The biggest steam turbines yet built," Leland boasted.

"Okay boys, here comes another statue," Carter prompted.

They were coming close to this one. It was covered in a patina, stained with corrosion, and in a few places white from bird guano.

The arm was extended and the hand pointed toward the port.

"Let commerce flow and weary travelers take respite," Leland read.

Tourists looked from the island at them as they passed. A few raised impression-boxes and took images as they went by.

Several ferryboats filled with tourists

approached the small pier. The wake of the Valliant
sent wave upon wave surging toward the ferries
causing the small boats to bob up and down with
great tempo. No one on those boats seemed to mind
though, as they climbed onto the boardwalk and
scurried toward the statue.

Leland approached the railing and put his
elbows on it. He looked out at the calm bay as the
ship chugged toward port; the dark blue waters, the
crisp afternoon sky, the birds careening above, all
indicative of a joyful moment. His excitement was
growing.

He'd learned about the city from his tutor,
Oland Vin Childs. Childs was from Kifi, a region
known for its scholars. The man spoke seven
languages, and was meticulous in his instruction.
Leland could almost hear the old man.

*Tiquan - the first deep water port open to
steam travel, the capital of Hurgray; population five
hundred and fifty two thousand; known for the trade
routes from Indo, Kree, and Spilton; borders the
Rema desert; industries are steam engines, fabric
manufacturing, iron works, and agro-business;
government is a Shelby Court system, with
Magistrates, Prefects, Judges, and a Triumvirate
ruling body elected every five years.*

"Another statue," Tommy said coming up
alongside Leland.

A massive lantern held in the statue's right
hand blazed out to sea. The surface of the lens was
larger than the pool at Leland's home, and the beam
of light cut across the ships masts as it passed. The
words came into view: *Let the light of Tiquan bear*

warning, and salvation. The letters were gold and blazed in the sunlight.

They were getting closer to the docks and the boatswain rang the bell to call all hands to their stations. Over the cone-shaped amplifier the captain's voice echoed.

"Raise the colors!"

Up the main mast two crewmen hoisted the flag; a black background with silver crosses from upper left, descending to the lower right. The flag ballooned out as the wind opened it fully. Two sailors passed Leland.

"Sandy, I know where we should go when we get liberty," one said.

The other said, "Do you mean the Pink Palace?"

"Exactly!"

Leland looked over at Tommy.

"When we get liberty, we should try the Pink Palace," he said.

Tommy shrugged. "Sure, what is it?"

"Uh… I'm not sure, but it must be a fun place if the crew is going there."

"Here's the last one," Carter called out.

The statue stood tall and straight with its arms wide as if waiting for an embrace.

"Be welcomed with brotherly love," Leland read aloud.

"Sounds like an amazing city." Tommy said as he looked back at the previous statues. "I sure hope they're not lying to us."

At a half mile from the docks the tugs took

over. They pushed and pulled the huge ship until it was snuggly tucked into its berth. The mooring lines were secured, the side hatches opened, and gangplanks lowered to the docks.

A two day process awaited as the sailors began unloading cargo. Leland knew this would go on day and night for the next forty eight hours. After that, return cargo would be loaded, fresh fuel stored, and the Valliant would again set off under a full head of steam back toward Millton Bay and his homeland of Pohl.

"Come on, get your gloves and let's get down into the hold and start netting cargo in compartment J," Tommy said.

"You'll make a splendid captain one day," Leland told him.

"And one day, you'll be a great boss," Tommy chuckled. "Now, let's get to work!"

Chapter 2

Report to High Command: Garland family under surveillance. Father and mother currently out with armed escort. Agents will maintain distance and wait for opportunity to secure the children. End report.

***

Ella's eyes narrowed. "What do you mean I can't go out?"

Her brother took a step away from her... it looked as if she might attack. "Father says you have to stay in the hotel until they return with the escort," he said. "Then you can go out... with the escort."

She leveled her imposing gaze at him.

"They're not returning until one in the morning tomorrow! How am I supposed to go out then?"

"Not my problem," Geris said. "Anyway, you're safer here inside the hotel. Why don't you invite Crystal or Genya to come up?" He hedged his way toward the open door. "You know, play some quambi or paint each other's toenails or something..."

She grabbed a vase and hurled it at his head. It missed by an inch and smashed against the wall splashing water and flowers everywhere.

"You're a man and you can go anywhere you want!" she screamed. "I can handle myself anywhere and in any situation," she yelled after him, as he ran through the door and down the hallway to the lift.

Ella stomped into the hall and saw him frantically pushing the signal-button for the lift-box. The corners of her mouth twisted up, as her anger ebbed. She huffed, turned on her heels and went back in, slamming the door behind her.

"By all the elements, I'll have a night out," Ella swore.

She reached for the call-tube, pulled out the cork, and raised the funnel to her lips. She cranked the handle, and a red light illuminated on the box.

"This is room six twenty... yes the Garland suite. I want to leave a note-gram for Crystal Haskil and Genya Hemp. Of course I want it hand delivered to their room. Take this down, meet me in my suite, seven of the evening, and bring gown and money."

She waited for the operator to respond.

"Yes, that will be fine. Also, take this down for suite five ten, the Geris Garland room. In all caps, please write— *Dear brother, mottel off and I hope you get a case of cankers while you're out tonight*... What do you mean you can't write that?"

Ella considered feigning outrage, then thought better of it.

"Okay, I understand. Don't worry about the last message. I'll do it myself."

She put down the funnel and replaced the cork. The red light blinked out, and she went to the secretary. Taking out a piece of white paper, she wrote in her best handwriting the obscene thoughts she meant for her brother. Carefully folding it she placed it in a small white envelope, sealed the flap with red wax, and kissed it on the front leaving dark red lip-paint on it.

"That'll get his attention." Ella chuckled, then went to the window.

Down below was the main street. Black cabs were numerous, as were men dressed in tweed jackets of every description. Their heads were adorned with round bowler hats or black topers. From time to time Ella saw women, their wide hoopskirts and magnificent walking-hats displayed like a homber bird's plumage.

Ella pined for those streets; after all, she'd been kept at the Garland country home since she was ten. Now, she was ready to experience all that magic her tutors had bragged about. She wanted to see Turner Park and walk there bathed in the yellow glow of the nighttime gas-lamps.

She wanted to have a beer in a tavern and dance at a *fine-house*. Most of all, she wanted to meet a mysterious stranger who would sweep her off her feet, take her about the city, hold her close at midnight, and kiss her under the green light of the moon.

Oh how her nerves tingled with the thought of such excitement. A knock at the door roused her, and she quickly unlocked it and threw the portal wide open. Crystal and Genya stood there, dress clothes in their hands and grins as big as window panes.

"I can't wait to get out there," said Genya.

"Maybe we'll all get boys tonight," Crystal mused.

"Come on, girls. We have makeup to put on and primping to do." Ella led the way to the bedroom and the vanity.

They snuck down the back stairs; six flights of black iron steps that led to a wrought iron gate. The three girls stepped into the ally, then down to and out onto the main boulevard walkway.

A loud bell cracked the air, the sound echoing down the street; the city tower rang eight of the evening. The clack of the carriage wheels ticked by, and the bustle of movement was all around them.

Ella's corset was tight. She barely kept air in her lungs, and the descent down the stairs had nearly winded her.

"Help me," she said to Genya, "and loosen my corset."

Genya unbuttoned Ella's dress in the back and slightly untied her bodice

"Ah, that's better. I can finally breathe." She filled her lungs with the city air, while her eyes scanned the street amidst the contrast of shadows and streetlight.

Men and women walked arm in arm. The men strolled along the curbside while the women were tucked away from the splashing spoke-wheels of passing cabs. Ella was instantly in love with the city.

"Where too?" Crystal asked.

Ella spun around and pointed. "That way." She happily skipped down the walkway to the intersection.

Crystal called out. "Where are we going?"

"I don't know yet!" Ella replied.

A black cab stopped, and the driver on top leaned down. Tipping his cap, he looked at the girls and smiled.

"Can I offer a cab to ya, girlies?" he said with a Carmenian accent.

"Just point us to the nearest tavern and we'll say good-night," Genya said while curtsying.

He eyed them for a moment, then accepted that they'd not be paying a fare for his cab.

"Could you direct us to the nearest place to dance and get drinks?" Ella asked.

"Ya go down dat street, cross ways to Wiggly Place. Ya can't miss it. Big sign says Breville Tavern. Best beer-drinks to be had and strong spirits too. A good place to twittle yer narbos lasses!" He chuckled then regarded them again. "Yer pretty little things. Lotta wicked types here in the city. Stay together if ya don't know these streets. Just saying ya should better keep yer wits."

The cabbie snapped the reins and pulled out into the busy street and vanished into a sea of horse drawn carts and buggies. The three girls looked at each other and giggled.

"Did you hear the way he spoke?" Crystal asked.

"Sounded like a Carmenian," said Ella. "No matter, let's get going before we're missed. I'm ready to have a drink at the Breville Tavern."

They crossed the street, weaving between slow moving cabs and carriages. Once across, they headed in the direction the cabbie had pointed. Three blocks later they came to Wiggly Place that intersected with Main Street. They stood in front of a large sign made of black letters over gold backing: *Breville Tavern and Lodgers Den.*

Ella went to the double brass-hinged doors and laid her hand on the handle just as the doors came open. Two men dressed in evening clothes stopped short and looked down at the girls. One man in a topper and black tie regarded them. He stepped aside while tipping his hat.

"Pardon," said the man.

His friends did the same and they gave way for the girls to enter.

"Nice fellows," Crystal said, as she passed into the red and gold interior.

The hallway was twenty feet long and lined with red carpet. The walls were covered in gold paper with fleur de lis patterns up and down it. On the ceiling, stamped copper accents adorned the roof, and gas lights illuminated all in a yellow hue.

They moved out into the floor space where tables and diners sat. Ella saw the dance floor - men in formal dress with their counterparts hard at work gliding, whirling, and sashaying over the alabaster surface to the tune of Old Jinx played by an orchestra.

"A table, my ladies?" a man in a white tuxedo asked.

"Yes, down toward the front," Ella said.

The man nodded. "It might be a while. Those tables are often reserved."

"I'm Ella Garland—daughter of Emerald Garland, the shipping baron."

The waiter looked unimpressed. "I'll see what I can do. In the meanwhile, you may wish to wait in the bar." He pointed to an alcove where double doors upholstered in red leather were closed. "Just through there," he added with a gesture of his hand.

***

Leland put on his leather belt, his holster dangling from the right side. He strapped the leg cord around his thigh and tied it. The Corbit pistol was fully charged with eight rounds of ninety percent hydrogen peroxide.

His father had given it to him when he turned seventeen. An excellent piece of craftsmanship— custom polished oak grip, brass frame, steel cylinder etched with his crest and name. Not only did it look impressive, it was quite functional too.

"What do you need that for?" Tommy frowned.

"Better than carrying a saber." Leland pointed at the sword and baldric Tommy had slung over his shoulder.

"Ya, but the law in Tiquan don't mind a man to carry a saber, but does to carrying a pistol. Didn't you read the rules?"

Leland nodded. "It's under my coat. No one will even know."

"If you wind up in the prison here, your dad will have my dad's job," Tommy angrily said.

"Don't worry. No one's going to find out. Anyway, if we get beset by a few unruly fellows, a couple of shots from this peroxide shooter will send 'em scurrying."

Shaking his head, Tommy moved toward the

door. He stopped and looked back. "You better make sure nothing happens," he said, as he opened the door and stepped into the hallway.

Leland followed. Two older men in formal black jackets were coming down the hallway. One regarded the two young men as they passed but said nothing. Reaching the lift, Tommy pressed the button and they waited.

A woman approached leading a small six-legged bander on a long leather leash. The creature snorted and growled.

"Going out, boys?" She looked them both over with an expression of mild amusement.

"Yes, ma'am," Leland said with a slight bow. "Do you know the Pink Palace?"

She gave a knowing grin. "Not a place for such gentlemen as you. You'll have better luck at the Breville. I think if you give the bar a sit, you'll find what you're looking for."

A bell rang, and the doors to the lift opened.

A man in a short waistcoat and red dress slacks controlled the elevator lever. "What floor?" he asked.

"Lobby," Leland said then motioned for the lady to enter.

The woman entered and made sure her pet was in, then added, "The same for me."

Leland and Tommy followed and the doors closed.

As the box descended, Tommy looked at the older lady. "Pardon me for asking, but where might we find the Breville?"

"Main and Wiggly Place. It's on the corner.

The bottom floor is a tavern and dining room. The upper floors are the hotel. A respectable establishment."

The lift stopped, and the doors opened. She walked out as her bander led the way.

Leland stepped out onto the polished marble floor - a milky white contrasted by stripes of black onyx laid at angles extending to the brass double doors at the entrance.

Tommy followed, but broke off at an angle to the reception desk. He stopped there for a moment, and then met Leland at the doors.

"What was that all about?" Leland asked.

Tommy shrugged. "I wanted to see if there were any messages for us."

"Was there?"

"There wasn't." He looked at Leland's long coat. "Looks like you're carrying a gun with that bulge at the side of you jacket."

"Don't worry about it," Leland said. "Now, let's find some action."

**

Men mingled freely, drinking and laughing all around the bar. Ella and her friends sat in a red and gold booth along one wall, sipping pink galleons. Several men approached asking if the women would dine with them, but the girls were aloof, turning down each suitor and sending them away with a shake of the head.

Crystal was about to say something when two men entered the bar. Both were handsome, and well dressed—not in traditional formal attire, but smart tweed coats and well-pressed wool trousers.

One stopped and looked around.

Ella's curiosity was piqued. She studied them. One was six feet tall, lean and muscular, with sapphire blue eyes. The other was a little shorter, muscular and stout, with dark hair and gold-brown eyes.

The closest one removed his outlander hat to reveal golden-blond hair. He tucked the hat under his arm. The other man removed his derby and they found a place at the bar to sit.

Ella smiled. "Those lads are snarkly," she said, motioning to them.

Crystal craned her neck and looked in the direction of Ella's gaze. "Those two?" She eyed them for a moment. "They are very snarkly indeed."

Genya looked, then frowned. "There's only two." She glanced at Crystal. "We'll have to double up." She sipped her drink and then giggled.

Ella chuckled. "Sharing a man is easier than marrying one."

Genya snickered as she ogled the young fellows.

***

"Those girls over there keep looking at us," Tommy said.

Leland glanced over and shrugged. "Fine looking ladies."

Tommy lifted his drink to his lips and sipped the strong spirit.

"They're looking again," repeated Tommy.

Leland glanced over. One of the girls met his gaze, and her emerald eyes blazed. He sat transfixed for a moment. It seemed that all the noise in the bar fell silent, and the patrons vanished as he saw only the girl in the white dress with pink lace.

His heartbeat quickened as if he'd taken a full dose of hequin dust. She stared back, then shyly smiled. The spell broke and the rush of sound and pandemonium erupted around him again.

"Okay, don't answer me!" Tommy snapped.

"What? I didn't hear you."

Tommy smirked, then chuckled. "I see that. I said, let's get out of here and go to the Pink Palace."

"Why be so hasty? Let's see what transpires here with these ladies in that booth."

Leland stood and swaggered over to the women.

"Hi, ladies. My name's Leland, and that's my friend Tommy," he said, pointing back at Tommy. He waved his friend over. "We would love it if all three of you would join us for supper."

Ella looked up with a coy smile. "My name is Ella, and this is Crystal and Genya." She nodded to her friends. "I'm pleased to make your acquaintance." She put out her hand. Leland took it and kissed it.

Tommy approached and shyly looked down at his boots. "We're waiting for a table," he said.

"How about it? Would you ladies like to dine with us?" Leland produced his very best smile.

"I'm sorry, but we hardly know you," said Crystal. "We can't be expected to just take up with the first Johnny-hoody who comes along, now can we?"

Leland bowed slightly. "Well then…" He

turned and walked back to the bar, grabbed two stools and returned. "We'll just have to get to know one another." He sat down across from Ella.

Tommy flushed red. He'd never been so embarrassed before.

"Lee, what are you doing? They said they don't want to have supper with us." Tommy pulled at Leland's jacket sleeve.

Leland brushed his hand away. "I'll not be clawed at like a jinx over a beetrun carcass. Until these ladies tell me to bugger off, I'm going to get to know them."

Ella giggled. Crystal and Genya both smiled at Leland's impetuousness.

Ella waved over the bartender. "Please sir, fill the order of these two gentlemen with whatever they desire, and put it on my bill."

The barkeep looked down at the two men and raised his eyebrows in expectation.

"Oh, I'll have four fingers of Old Stewart," Tommy said.

Leland looked across at Ella; he was getting used to the sudden pace of his heart. "You wouldn't happen to have a drink called an Ella, would you?"

The bartender looked deep in thought. "I can't say that I've ever heard of such a thing. What's in it?"

"One part deep and abiding love, and two parts unbridled passion, topped with a night of dancing," Leland said.

"Just tell me what drink you want, sonny!" the bartender said while rolling his eyes.

"I'll have four fingers of Old Stewart too."

The barkeep left and quickly returned with the two glasses of liquor. He turned and walked away without comment.

Leland took a sip. "So, tell me ladies, where are you from?"

Ella spoke first. "I'm from a city called Maguay in Ciciro."

"We're all from there," Genya added. "Where are you two from? It must be a place where the wishes of respectable women are not heeded." She smiled while stirring her drink with a small wooden rod.

"I have a home near Milton Bay," said Leland.

"Both of us live there," Tommy told them. "It's really a beautiful place."

"You're both from the Phol Empire?" Ella asked, her smile vanishing.

Leland frowned. "Is that a problem? I hope that doesn't offend you?"

Ella's smile returned. "No, that's actually thrilling."

Crystal and Genya both looked at her.

It was clear to Leland and Tommy that there was something else going on – perhaps some taboo that they'd violated.

Ella glared at her two friends and then turned back to Leland, smiling very sweetly. "Don't worry, we're all three thrilled to be meeting some handsome men from Phol."

"Okay." Leland chuckled and turned to Ella. "What is it you do for fun?"

"Oh, any manner of things," Ella replied.

"Like?" Tommy scooted his stool closer.

"Mount ridding, taking long trips on steam-wheels, the occasional ship ride, the ballet, the opera, and the theater…" Ella looked at her friends. "Am I leaving anything out?"

Crystal giggled. "I don't think so."

"You forgot the parties," Genya corrected.

"Oh my, how could I have forgotten the garden parties and the balls," said Ella. "How about you two?"

"Very much the same," Leland said, "very similar pursuits indeed."

Crystal put her gloved hand out on the table near Tommy's arm. "Don't you just find my new gloves the Torrid's Coals?"

"I do."

"Go ahead, feel the quality of the fabric," she said, goading Tommy to touch her hand.

He reached out and gingerly felt the material. It was smooth, cool, and soft. He felt uncomfortable as his blood felt like it was boiling in his veins.

She pulled back her hand. "Spider silk from Petrah," Crystal said.

"Here Tommy, feel mine," Genya said as she put her hand on his knee.

Tommy jumped at the touch and nearly fell from his stool. Genya giggled softly.

"Very nice," Tommy clumsily said as he stroked her gloved hand.

"Which one do you like best?" Genya asked.

"Uh… I think I really like them both equally as well."

The two girls looked at each other, then back at Tommy.

Crystal fluttered her eyelashes at him. "Then I think we'll get along quite well."

Tommy felt like a tip-mouse in the clutches of a volereever, but the fact was, he liked this attention and craved much more.

"I'd like that very much," Tommy said with confidence.

Both girls giggled again.

Chapter 3

Report to High Command: Garland daughter has left the hotel. Opportunity is presented. Requesting authorization for action. End Report.

***

Ella, Crystal, Genya, Leland and Tommy danced late into the night. At first they all danced together, then slowly, Ella and Leland broke away and danced only with each other. By the time the waiters announced the *last-glass* at the bar, the five of them went to the parlor and sat near the fireplace.

"That was so much fun," Ella declared.

Leland warmed his hands by the flames. "It was, and I can't wait to do it again!"

Tommy was blocked in on the couch by Crystal and Genya, who sat eyeing him like candy.

"I could dance for another couple of hours..." Tommy looked at both girls. "Sadly we really need to get back. Lee and I have some work to do later today."

"Work?" Crystal looked disappointed.

"Aye, we both work for the Niva shipping company," Tommy said.

Genya folded her arms. "Niva? We thought you lads were gentlemen."

"Of a kind," Leland added. He regarded Ella for a moment then took up her hand in his and kissed it. "I'm quite sorry, but we do need to fly. If you promise to be here tonight, we will too."

"Perhaps we will," Ella said. "You'll just have to come and find out." She retracted her hand

and crossed her legs. She smiled. "Well, Mister *Leland* and Mister *Tommy*, though you work for a disreputable establishment as the Niva shipping company we have enjoyed *your* company and will consider your offer for another night out. Now, you may bugger off."

Leland chuckled. "You have sand, my lady – you have much sand."

"Let's get out of here," Tommy said standing and heading toward the door, then he ground to a halt as both Crystal and Genya had a hold of his coat tails. "What's this?"

Crystal and Genya stood up. Each kissed him on the cheek and then sat back down.

Tommy flushed. "What was that for?"

"You'll find out, if you come back tonight," Genya said.

"With mysterious words like that, it's guaranteed," said Tommy.

Leland stood up. "We'll be off. If you're not here later tonight, you'll not get a present that I'm going to buy you."

Ella raised her eyebrows. "What present?"

Leland bowed. "Until tonight," he said, then looked over at Crystal and Genya and added, "Ladies…" He turned and made for the door.

Crystal sat back; the last of her drink was pooled at the bottom of her glass. "I'm glad you didn't let your parents keep you pent up in that stuffy old suite."

"Speaking of that, we'd better get back. My parents were supposed to be at the hotel by one," Ella said. "If they find out I've absconded, we'll not get out of the hotel again the rest of this trip." All three girls made for the front door.

The air was cool and the streets mostly vacant. Ella walked arm-in-arm with Crystal and Genya. The street lamps washed their footsteps in soft yellow light, beating the darkness back to the buildings edges. Ahead was the street that led back to the hotel.

"That sure was super fun," Genya said as they turned the corner.

"Lots of fun say ya, little ladies?" a man's voice came from behind them.

The girls walked a little faster, but two men stepped out from a dark alley just ahead. Both wore battered and frayed bowler hats, ill-fitting dark coats, and threadbare trousers. One of them held a wooden axe handle, and the other produced a long shiny knife.

"Where you think you're going, my little dearies?" the man with the knife asked. He smiled and showed he lacked both front teeth as well as manners.

"Them's off to the ball, me thinks," the ruffian with the axe handle said, as he slapped the hardwood into his palm.

From across the street two men came. They were different, dressed in clean and expensive black trousers, black boots, long black split-tail coats, and black toppers.

"Is this the young Ms. Garland?" one of them said while tipping his hat. "I am enchanted at making your acquaintance, to be sure."

The other man also tipped his hat and bowed

slightly. "Truly a woman of much beauty," he said. "Please to let me introduce myself. I am Heinz Foltz, the adviser to the Burkmuran government here in Hurgray. I have been asked to seek you out and invite you to visit the Ambassador. Also, the invitation is extended to your lovely friends as well." He nodded to Genya and Crystal.

"What is this about?" Crystal demanded.

"All will be explained once we are at the embassy," Heinz said.

"And if we refuse to go," Ella challenged.

"Then we will take you by force, which is why we employed these fine gentlemen." He motioned with his hand to the goons surrounding the girls.

Ella moved quickly and kicked Heinz in the leg. The man fell to the side, and Ella shouted, "This way!"

The three girls ran toward a dark alley across the street. The hired goons were on their heels every step of the way. Ella dashed down the road between the high brick buildings only to find it blocked at the end with a wall and a wooden door. She turned and produced a small dagger. Swinging it from side to side, she nearly cut one of the ruffians.

"Now, me lovely, you don't want to go and do that do you?" said the lead tough.

"I'll gut the first of you that tries to lay a hand on us!" Ella shouted.

The two Burkmuran men arrived. Heinz pushed his way forward. The green moon was full, and in the dim light of the alley he shook his head.

"You're a pistol, my little sweet-pie," he said.

"No, actually I *have* a pistol, and I'll kill each of you if you don't step aside," Leland said loudly from behind.

"What's this?" Heinz turned around. "Who in the Height's Hell are you?"

"None of your business! Now step aside or you'll be the first to fall," Leland assured him.

"Ella, Crystal, Genya, come this way," Tommy said, his saber in his hand and ready for action.

Ella moved forward waving her dagger from side to side to make sure the men stayed out of the way. Once through, the girls ran out to the street.

"Come on," Ella shouted back, "let's get out of here!"

Leland and Tommy backed out to the street. "We can't have you following us, so…" Leland fired his pistol. The loud pop echoed in the alley, followed by a puff of steam as the peroxide weapon discharged.

A yelp filled the air, as one of the thugs fell to the ground clutching his leg.

"I want you to know that I'm serious. If any of you leave this alley in the next ten minutes, I'll kill him," Leland said, and backed around the corner.

Leland, Tommy and the girls flew down the street as fast as their feet could go.

"Who were those guys?" Tommy asked as they ran.

"I don't know, but one said he was with the

Burkmuran Embassy," Genya huffed.

They slowed down and started walking. Leland checked behind them. No one followed. He holstered his pistol and covered it with his coat.

"How did you find us?" Crystal asked, still out of breath.

"We realized that we were not being very good gentlemen leaving you women exposed to the street alone. So we were on our way back when we saw you walking away. You turned a corner and we rushed up to find you surrounded by those men," Leland said.

Ahead was the hotel - the gaslights illuminating the street just under the sign. Leland stopped and held Ella by the arm.

"Were they in the Breville?"

"I don't know. I guess they could have been; I just don't remember seeing any of them there," Ella said.

"Do you have any idea why a Burkmuran official would want you?" Tommy slid his sword back into its scabbard.

"No idea. They knew me though, like they were after me. What could they have wanted?" Ella looked down the street then at the hotel. "A most peculiar night."

"Best that you ladies notify the authorities. Make a report in the morning. Tommy and I will see you tomorrow, and this time we won't just leave you to the Tiquan streets. Sorry about that."

Ella smiled. "That's okay. Those fellows back there were taught a lesson – wouldn't you say?" She chuckled while sheathing her dagger back into its hiding place under her dress.

Leland reached out and took Ella by the waist pulling her into him. He leaned into her. She leaned into him. Their lips came together as he kissed her, and she kissed him back.

Ella broke off and stepped back. "You cheeky bastard," she said. "Maybe next time I should keep my dagger at hand around you too."

"If you didn't like my kiss, then take that dagger and drive it into my heart, for I'm loath to live if I've done something to offend you." Leland pushed his chest out.

Ella smiled, and all three girls laughed. "You do have sand," she said. "Come on girls, let's get to our rooms." She turned and started walking into the light toward the doorman.

He opened the doors and tipped his hat as the girls entered. Ella stopped and turned back.

"Tomorrow, where we agreed!" she called into the street.

Leland looked on as she vanished into the brilliant glow of the building's lobby. He glanced back down the street, then slapped Tommy on the shoulder.

"Come on, let's get out of here before those toughs come looking for us."

***

"Leland," shouted Carter as he strode across the deck. "Your father is in Hurgray. I received a note-gram just now instructing me to bring you to him."

"Did it say why?" Leland looked confused.

Carter motioned for Leland to follow him to the gangplank.

"No. All it says is that I am to bring you immediately to West Pincer Abbey House in the country. If we're to make the next steam-wheeler, we'll have to hurry."

They both walked quickly down the plank to the docks. Carter hailed a cab and instructed the man to get them to Central Terminal post-haste.

The cab took off like a shot and maneuvered through the crowded streets. Leland watched as the harbor warehouses gave way to slum housing, then to industrial factories.

Further on came the middle class lots with three-story homes and wide yards. The cab crossed the trolley tracks many times and transitioned into the center of the city. The city streets were packed with busy men traveling to and from their business dealings.

The Harper and Collins Trade building stood five stories tall and was bustling with men in black long coats and toppers. Some wadded the front stairs to the high marble entrance; others exited plodding down the stairs toward waiting cabs. Next to it was the Tiquan Public Seat, the place where the magistrates meet to deal with the laws of the land.

The cab turned onto a long avenue; to either side Leland saw long stone troughs with running water in them. Again the cab turned and they were heading toward the large and imposing Central Terminal, the main steam-wheel station for the city.

"Here ya are, matties. It'll be a forkal for me trouble," the cabbie said.

Carter paid him and stepped down onto the walkway. Leland followed.

"Come on!" Carter said, as he ran to the ticket office and paid for two tickets. Leland ran alongside as Carter dashed down the iron and red-brick platform.

The large black engine and drive frame of the steam-wheel came into view. The giant brass cog directly behind the pilot's control house was fitted into the center track. The two outer wheels were far forward, set on the outer tracks. Two black smoke stacks were angled from the main furnace to vent the smoke away from the control house, and the center boiler churned with boiling water.

A loud chime echoed from the platform clock, as the pilot stuck his head out of the control house window and shouted, "Last call to get aboard!"

Carter jumped onto the loading-steps just as the line of cars jolted forward. Leland grabbed onto the steel handle by the door and climbed up as the cars began moving down the track. The roof supports for the platform began moving quickly past as the steam-wheel cars picked up speed.

Carter wiped his brow with his handkerchief. "That was close." He turned and opened the door into the car and found a seat.

Leland sat down opposite Carter and looked out the window as the landscape began to change from station buildings and rail yards, to city industrial spurs connected to large, dark structures.

"Do you suppose we'll be back before nightfall?" Leland asked.

"Possibly. It depends on what your father wants." Carter pulled out a small book from his jacket pocket and opened it. "Now, settle in… we have an hour or so before we get to the town of Burly Wood."

As the steam-wheel docked at Burly Wood Station, Carter pulled out his pocket watch and noted the time. "Early afternoon… I think we'll most likely make it back to Tiquan before night fall."

They walked through the terminal and out onto the town street. Here, the colloquial dress was common, and the stalwart smell of burning coal and manure filled the air.

Carter hailed a cab. "Take us to West Pincer Abbey House."

They climbed into the carriage. The driver cracked his whip and the rig headed north along a dirt road.

After a time, the cab came over a rise and around a grove of trees, where West Pincer Abby House came into view. It was a massive house, five stories tall with towers at the corners rising to seven stories. The dusky yellow stone reflected the sun making the structure appear golden.

"How many rooms is this place?" Leland asked.

"I've heard it can cater to a party of a thousand people, but I don't know the exact number of rooms," Carter said.

"Well, it does look like a hotel," Leland added.

They arrived at the front door and climbed down from the carriage. Two automatic steam-powered stalk slicers were cutting the grass, while a vigilant grounds keeper kept watch. A butler came from the door and gave a slight bow.

"Lord Bowland is expecting you both in the library. Please follow me."

They were led through the main hall; marble floors and tall columns were illuminated by the many gas lights. Wooden chairs gilded in gold and upholstered in red satin were placed along the walls and near the large fireplace.

The butler moved down a hallway and stopped at two fifteen-foot-high white doors. Opening them, he motioned for Leland and Carter to enter. The doors closed behind, and they found themselves in the presence of a resplendent three-story library.

At one end Leland saw a wide hardwood desk with chairs. Behind the desk were rows and rows of books lining shelves that extended to the second floor. Brass railings and several ladders on rollers gave the appearance of a city library.

"Ah, I see that you've arrived," said a man who was sitting behind the desk. He stood and walked around the table. "Come in and have a seat."

Franz Niva stood up from a high-backed brown leather chair and motioned for them to come near.

"We have a situation," Franz began. "Lord Bowland has informed me that Hurgray will soon be at war with Burkmuran. He has suggested that we take our ships out of the harbor as soon as possible."

"War?" Leland said surprised. "What?"

Franz looked as if he was embarrassed by the question. "Excuse my son, he is green when it comes such matters," he said to Lord Bowland.

Lord Bowland nodded but said nothing.

"How much time do we have?" Carter asked.

"Not much, I'm afraid. The Count of Burkmuran was murdered on the island of Palitz two days ago. As you know the island is under the protection of Hurgray. The Ambassador of Burkmuran demanded that Hurgray denounce the act and give up authority of Palitz. Hurgray has refused, and Burkmuran has declared war."

Lord Bowland cleared his throat. "I have it on good authority that four dreadnaughts are speeding toward Tiquan harbor. If they blockade the port, your ships will be locked in for the duration."

"I'll get right back and take our ships out to sea," Carter said.

"Make sure that my son is on the first ship out of here. Get back to Milton Bay. I have to meet with the Triumvirate of Hurgray. They have asked that the Phol Empire aid them against this aggression. As a Party representative of the Empire I have a duty to consult with this government. It is unclear at the moment who is allied with Burkmuran, but if they do get supporters, we in the south will have no choice but to form an alliance. This will be a messy business."

Franz turned and walked to a decanter sitting on a small round table. He poured two glasses with an amber liquor, took one and handed the other to Lord Bowland. Carter and Leland looked at one another then back at Franz.

"Sorry boys, I'd offer you some whisky, but you have to get back to Tiquan, and you'll need to keep your wits about you."

***

Mister Garland marched up and down in front of Ella, Crystal, and Genya. His rage was unleashed, and he scolded them about leaving the hotel.

"Do you know how dangerous it is outside, and how dishonest it was for you to disobey me?" he shouted.

Just as he was launching into a second rant the doorbell rang, and a messenger was brought to him. He took the note-gram and read it. His angry face changed to confusion, then he spoke.

"I'll be back. None of you are to leave this room until I return!"

He grabbed his coat, topper, and cape and left with his bodyguard. The door closed, and the women all looked at each other.

"What do you suppose that was about?" Mrs. Garland asked.

"Very strange indeed," Ella added.

Geris walked out of the back bedroom. "I heard the shouting stop. Where's Father?"

"He had to leave, and didn't say why." Crystal sat down on the couch and looked across the room at the large windows that overlooked the city. "Most unusual to say the least."

"There aren't many people out on the street

tonight," Geris looked out of the windows as the sound of thunder echoed in the distance. "I think we're in for a shower or two."

"Don't be stupid," Ella snapped. "There isn't even a cloud in the sky, how could there be rain?"

Geris shrugged and sat at the wet-bar. "It could be a storm coming in from the ocean." A white flash of light from the harbor illuminated the room. He pointed out the window. "See, there's lightning." The shock of the thunder rattled the windows.

Ella went to the bar and shook her head. "Ridiculous!"

She poured herself a glass of port and sat on one of the stools next to her brother.

"It must be a reflection from the street... or something else." Ella froze as she looked out the window as a flash lit up the sky followed by another boom. "I'll be dipped in tar. You're right, there seems to be a storm coming." She sipped her drink.

Several booms echoed one right after the other. Mrs. Garland approached the window and stared out. Her features became pale and she sat down.

"That's not thunder," Mrs. Garland said. "It's exploding shells." She looked at the others, "The harbor is being attacked."

***

The steam-wheel arrived at Central Terminal and came to a halt. The sound of thunder had made Leland dawn his coat. Once at the terminal he saw men in uniform rushing about.

"What's going on?" Leland shouted from the car window.

"We're under attack. The forces of Burkmuran have landed at the harbor," one of the uniformed men shouted back.

Carter's face fell. "We have to get you out of here," he said.

"Look," Leland pointed, "it's Tommy."

Tommy rushed along the platform. In his hand was a bag and on his back a pack. Several other sailors from the ship were with him. The men made their way across the platform to a set of stairs leading down to the tracks.

Carter dashed from the cabin, rushed out and shouted. "Tommy!"

Tommy stopped and looked back, his expression of extreme stress changed to visible relief. "Father!" Tommy called back.

The two men met on the tracks as Carter hugged his son. Leland disembarked and rushed over too. Carter looked at his boy.

"What in Height's Hell is happening?" he asked.

Tommy was overwhelmed with emotion as tears came to his eyes. "They sank the Valliant right there at the docks. We didn't have a chance to get her under steam." He fell to the side and sat down on the center track. "I tried, Dad – I tried to get the engine room hatch open, but it was jammed. I heard the men crying out to open it…" He sobbed for a moment. "I couldn't get it open… the water was everywhere."

Carter grabbed Tommy by the shoulders and

pulled him up. "Get on your feet, son. I know your sadness, but we have to get on the move." He turned to Leland. "We have to get out of here, post haste. Find what train is heading outbound. Anyplace outside the city will do. Meet me up there on the platform."

Leland took off at a run. Carter climbed up onto the platform. Tommy and the other sailors followed. They all gathered around Carter.

"Listen up lads, we've got to get clear of this fight and get across the southern isthmus to Port Hyde. If the Burkmuran soldiers catch you, don't give 'em a fight. They'll probably just dump you at the border and send you on your way. It's not worth your life to resist."

Leland skidded to a halt at Carter. "I saw three engines making ready to leave. The 444 is heading south across the isthmus; I figured we'd head that way to get to Hyde."

Carter smiled. "I couldn't have thought it out better myself."

Leland pointed at a steam-wheel engine two platforms away; a white painted wrought iron plate with the raised numbers 444 shone in the yellow gaslight.

"There," Leland said.

They moved toward the passenger cars attached to the 444 engine. The popping sound of gunfire erupted, and soldiers rushed toward the station entrance. Loud cracking sounds filled the air, and explosions shook the ground. Leland fell to the side and struggled to his feet. Across the platform he saw Ella, Crystal and Genya. Ella was getting back up and dusting off her dress. He broke away and ran across an engine berth, climbed the steps and halted a few feet from her.

"Ella!" Leland shouted. "What are you doing here?"

She looked over with surprise. "Leland?" She stepped back just as a bullet ricocheted off one of the iron beams supporting the mezzanine roof. Two large toughs took Leland to the ground.

"Unhand that boy," Carter said as he arrived.

The two large men stepped away, and Carter helped Leland up.

"What are you up to? We're in the middle of a war and you're running around like a fool!" Carter chided Leland.

"This is Ella, a girl I met the other night," Leland said.

Another explosion shook the platform. In the distance the sound of buzzing was growing nearer.

Leland turned to Ella. "What are you doing here?"

She turned back to the people she was with. "We're trying to get the mottle out of here!"

"We're going south toward the isthmus, come with us," Leland said.

An older man stepped forward. "Toward Port Hyde? Good idea. We have at least four freighters there loading supplies."

"Mister Garland?" Carter asked, surprised.

"Do I know you?" Mr. Garland leaned forward and adjusted his pince-nez.

"My name is Carter Wayne; I work for the Niva shipping company. We met at the Shifton conference to discuss design innovations in turbine manufacturing. I'm sorry we have to meet again under these circumstances."

A whistle blew from the 444.

"Is Franz here in the city?" Mr. Garland asked.

"No sir, but I must insist that if we're to get out of here, we'd better get to that steamer at a quick step." Carter pointed to the steam-wheel.

"Yes, I agree. We can sort this out later." A barrage of bullets flew past them. The buzzing was growing loud.

They all ran to the train and boarded. As Leland got on, he looked toward the entrance and saw the steel-blue uniforms of the Burkmuran soldiers spreading out.

The steam-wheel moved and the cars clanked together. He held onto the metal railing as the car lurched forward, then he went inside. The cars picked up speed as the enemy rushed toward them. Rifles were raised and shouts were made, but the steam-wheel pilot made no attempt at slowing. The chain of cars exited the station. Leland heard an explosion behind him. He craned his neck at the window to see behind. Black smoke and fire were dancing together like hellish demons.

Airships were numerous, and he watched as a large one passed overhead. A bomb fell directly behind them and the wave from its detonation washed over the cars.

He fell to the side, then forward, then

between two seats. The sound of metal tearing and wood shattering filled the air. For a moment he was dazed as he struggled to get to his feet. Everything was sideways.

Struggling over the seat he found Ella. She rubbed her head.

"What in the mottle happened?"

Carter wove his way through the debris. "We've been knocked off the tracks. We got to get out of here."

The smell of smoke filled the air.

"Quick, up to the door." He helped Leland and Ella out of the burning car.

Tommy followed as did the others. Last to leave was Carter.

Flames licked at his coat as he jumped to the ground. Behind them the city station was a shambles. Down a ways the steam-wheel cars were off the track and jumbled like children's wooden blocks carelessly scattered about.

The injured, wide-eyed, shaky and pale from the experience, shambled out and onto the scared sod.

"Look!" Tommy shouted.

From the city there was a distinct line of soldiers heading their way. One was yelling at them.

Mr. Garland limped over. His leg bloody, and holding a handkerchief over the wound, he nodded to Carter.

"Get my children from here, and I'll see that you are paid handsomely."

Ella ran to him. "No, I won't leave you and Mother."

Mrs. Garland approached. She was disheveled but okay.

"Your father is right. You, Crystal, Genya, and Geris need to go - now. Who knows what these Burkers have in mind? Your father and I will be okay. Go!"

Ella stepped back. More shouts were coming from the soldiers. They were three hundred yards and closing.

Carter pointed at a break in the cars. "Follow me," he said and led them through the wreckage.

More bombs erupted behind them, as the airships flew in an orbit around the city. A whistle blared into the air. Carter passed through a dense layer of acrid smoke and stumbled out onto another set of tracks. From the wrecked station a steam-wheel broke out, driving six cars wildly ahead of it.

Burker soldiers who were on the tracks jumped to the side to keep from being killed. Shots from the soldiers assailed the steam-wheel engine as it passed the belligerents. Bombs landed all around it, but the steam-wheel engine drove on.

"That's our way out," Carter shouted, as he ran to intercept the cars.

The vehicle slowed down, a man poked his head out from the pilothouse and shouted to them. "Get on, hurry!"

Carter lifted Ella, Genya, and then Crystal onto the running board of the last car as they all chased after it. Geris leapt on, then Tommy, and Leland. A peppering of gunfire hit the car and Leland fell back. There was some blood on his shirt.

He checked himself. Running his hand over his chest he realized the blood was not his. Looking down he saw Carter struggling to grab onto the railing. His arm was bloody.

The cars began to pull away. Carter was not going to make it. Tommy rushed to the running board, and Leland grabbed hold of him.

"Father!" Tommy shouted.

"Go on. Protect those you're with!" Carter slowed down from his run; the wheel-engine was passing him. "I'll see you soon enough!" He stopped running.

"We have to go back," Tommy shouted.

Leland looked gravely at Tommy. "We can't! They're trying their best to kill us all…"

Sitting down as the cars picked up speed and the wind blasted him, Tommy shook his head.

"Why, why…?" was all he kept saying.

Leland looked back toward Carter. Blue uniforms swarmed around him as the steam-wheel drove the cars around a bend, past a host of side-tracked cars, then out into the rural farmland that made up the eastern boarder of the city. In a matter of minutes they were careening at fifty miles an hour through wheat and barley fields.

As the sun was setting, an eerie red glow filled the western sky. In the distance Leland saw the shadowy shapes of large and small airships, and single winged flyers. He couldn't see the skyline of the city any longer, but he heard the explosions. He helped Tommy to his feet and into the car.

It was a luxury cabin, and the girls were already sitting on the couches. Ella had a decanter of whisky in her shaking hand and was sipping it.

"What happened to that other man?" Crystal asked.

"His name is Carter Wayne," Leland said, "and he was shot—"

"Dear lord!" Genya cried.

"He's still alive. They just winged him, but he couldn't hold onto the railing. We lost him to the soldiers." Leland glanced at each person in the car.

Ella looked up, tears welling in her eyes. "Do you think they'll kill my father?" Further words failed her.

Leland thought for a second then said, "I'm sure your parents have been taken as diplomatic hostages by now. I don't think they'll be hurt." He sat down on the floor as the clack of the wheels echoed all around.

"Carter is Tommy's father," Leland added as he looked over at his friend. Tommy's eyes were wet. "And he is a good friend to me and my family. He won't be harmed, I'm sure of it. Once the four of you are safe, I'll—"

"What? You're going to go back and rescue him?" Geris asked, a doubting look on his face. "You'll end up in the clink with him."

He came over and took the decanter from Ella and took a long swig, then handed the container to Leland. "No, if anything I should… we should make our way to Port Hyde and try and get back to Ciciro. I'm sure the word about Hurgray's trouble has made it there over the wire by now. Our battleships will be in route and those Burkers will have some atonement to make."

"Shut up, Geris," Ella said angrily. "Can't you see that these two fine lads have lost someone close to them too?" She turned back to Leland and Tommy. "I'm sure your dad will be okay." She watched as Genya put her arm around Tommy. Ella turned to Leland. "So, how do you know Tommy's father?"

"Tommy's my best friend," Leland said. "He and his dad work for my dad."

"Who's your father?" Ella raised her eyebrows in question.

"Franz Niva."

Ella stood up. "You're Franz Niva's son!" She looked at Crystal and Genya, then at Geris. "Your father's shipping company has been the bane of my family's business for two generations." She chuckled. "I guess if those Burkers had captured this car, they'd have gotten quite a prize; the children of four of the most powerful families on the Augerland Continent."

"Four families?" Leland asked.

"Crystal is heiress to the Haskil textile fortune. Genya is the daughter of Greely Hemp, the steel baron of Dutch. Including you, me, and my brother there," she pointed with her thumb at Geris, "we're all worth a pretty penny."

Leland narrowed his eyes. "Or could be used as leverage," he added. He was quiet for a moment, then looked out the window. The purple light of darkness was peppered with white sparkling stars. He took a sip from the decanter and handed it back to Geris, then stood up, walked to the door, and looked out along the track toward the city.

"What the mottle is happening?" he said softly, as the wind howled around him.

He saw black smoke pouring from the steam-wheel's firebox vents. Glittering far off in the distance were the running lights of the airships, and the flashes from their deadly cargo illuminating the skyline.

The car clacked loudly and swayed. He reached and grabbed onto the railing. There was something wet there, and he pulled back his hand. Blood was on his palm. His heart pumped strongly in his chest as if he'd run a mile.

He sat down on the car's platform. For a moment emotion overcame him and he sobbed. The wind of the speeding car felt good on his face as his hair whipped about. He stood up, wiped his hand on his shirt, then brushed the tears from his eyes and went back inside.

To his surprise Tommy was surrounded by Crystal and Genya, both of whom were caressing his hair and looking into his eyes. Leland smiled, then noticed Ella looking at him.

"You'd better sit down, before you fall down." She scooted over on the blue velvet couch and patted the spot next to her. "No reason we shouldn't at least be comfy."

Chapter 4

*Report to High Command: Invasion of
Tiquan disrupting efforts to find the Garland and
Niva youth. Agent reports that Leland Niva and five
others boarded a rogue steam-wheel moving east.
Will link up with Eastern Force Ergon and pursue.
End Report.*

***

Ella's eyes came open. She was lying on her side with her right arm draped over Leland's chest. A bolt of terror washed over her as she began to remember the events of the day before, and where she was. She took in a deep breath and exhaled slowly to calm herself.

Leland was warm, pressed against her legs, pelvis, and breasts. For a moment her thoughts turned to him.

She forgot her fear. Her imagination drifted as she envisioned Leland and her in a lover's bed at the Hilmore Hotel in Maguay. The car's wheels clacked loudly and shook the conveyance.

Leland groaned, then slowly sat up. He rubbed his eyes, and looked around. The warmth that drove Ella's fantasy swiftly vanished and she realized how cold the air was.

"Where are we?" Leland asked.

"I don't know." Ella sat up next to Leland and looked at a clock on the wall illuminated by a gas light. "It's near four in the morning."

Leland stood and walked to the dark

window. "Looks like a forest out there. What area of Hurgray has large forests?" he asked himself. "The foothills do… We must have been heading east all night." He looked around. Tommy, Genya, and Crystal were missing. "Where are Tommy and the girls?"

Geris sat forward. He'd been sleeping on one of the soft, over-stuffed chairs.

"I think I heard the connecting door open and close around one this morning."

"How'd you know it was one?" Ella asked.

"I heard the chime from the clock," Geris said and scowled.

Leland's belly growled and he looked embarrassed. "Sorry," he mumbled.

"That's okay, I think we're all a bit famished," Ella added.

The door to the connecting car came open and Tommy, Genya, and Crystal came through. Tommy held a tray with pastries on it, while Crystal and Genya carried a tea kettle, a box of tea and some cups.

The car shook as the steam-wheel made a turn. Genya staggered to the side and braced herself against the wall, as Crystal crouched down so as not to let the cups fall. Tommy tripped forward, but was caught by Geris who eased him into a chair.

"That was close," Geris said. "I'd better lighten your load." He grabbed up an éclair and took a big bite.

"Where did you find all that?" Leland asked.

"It was in the dining car just ahead. They had rows of them all laid out in the butler pantry.

We found tea and other stuff too," Tommy said.

"Any sign of the pilot?" Ella asked.

"Not so far," Tommy replied. "He's probably still in the pilothouse."

"Maybe we should take him something to eat," Ella suggested.

"Good idea," Leland agreed. "I'll take it to him. Maybe then I can find out how long it is to the next city."

He took two éclairs and wrapped them in a handkerchief. Next, he took a cup of tea, and then went to the doorway at the back of the car where the engine connected. As he exited, a cool wind blasted him causing his blond hair to fly about.

Unhooking the safety chain, he stepped out between the steam-wheel power plant and the car.

The tracks were speeding by in the darkness as he moved along the boiler toward the pilothouse and the massive single push wheel. Heat from the boiler tank was extremely warm and by the time he reached the door, he felt overcooked on his right, and undercooked on his left.

Flipping up the latch, he opened the door inward and stepped into the pilothouse.

It was dark, and the firebox illuminated the room with an eerie, orange glow. In the corner he saw the shape of a man sitting on a keg with a shovel between his knees and his head leaned back.

Leland sat the tea and éclairs down on a round pressure valve. He crept toward the man, not sure if he was alive or dead. Slowly, he became aware that there were holes in the wooden walls and the door of the pilothouse. His lips became tense and drawn as he realized that this man who'd saved them was dead.

A piercing whistle sounded; the man leapt up, drove his shovel into the coal box and heaped three scoops of the black fuel into the firebox before he realized that Leland was standing there wide-eyed and in shock.

"You okay, boy?" the man asked loudly to overcome the noise of the machinery. "You look as though you've seen ole Height himself."

Leland stepped back, his heart pounding in his chest. "You're not dead!" he choked out.

"Nope! Not dead; not yet. Those soldier-boys will have to do better than that to do me in. Boy they were mad as buzzing grieves when I brained one feller with my shovel and threw the forward switch all the way over. You should have seen 'em!" He laughed loudly. "Oh, I guess you did a bit later." He reached over and turned a small valve and the yellow glow of a light made all visible. "I see you brought something for me." He pointed at the bundle and tea cup.

"Yes sir. I thought you could use a bite and a cup of chi."

Leland saw the man clearly now. A head taller than he was, wearing a red striped cap that framed his soot covered face. The man smiled and his white teeth made a dramatic contrast to the coal dust on his cheeks.

"Right you were to think that. Those soldiers back there interrupted my supper. What'd you bring me?"

"Some éclairs," Leland said.

The man took the handkerchief and opened it. He quickly devoured the contents and took up the teacup. "Damn sporting of you to think of me like that. Thank you." He sipped the tea. "There were more of you. How many got on board?"

"There's six of us that we know of."

"That you know of?" The man adjusted a turn-valve, examined a couple of gages, tapped one, then sat back on the keg. "Those airships nearly blasted us to the next kingdom," he said and chuckled.

"Speaking of kingdoms, where are we heading?" Leland examined one of the bullet holes in the door.

"This track ends at Jutland. There's a roundhouse there that turns the steam-wheel around. Hopefully the Burkers haven't made it there yet. If they haven't, we stand a fair chance at getting over the mountains and down to Harrow's Gate. It's the start... or rather the finish... of the Silk Road that crosses the deserts. If we make it there, we can skirt the desert along the mountains toward Helsink."

"Helsink?" Leland said. "That's where we need to get to."

"I'm Cobain," the man said, offering his hand.

"I'm Leland Niva," Leland added and gripped tightly.

"Niva you say?" He stood up, let go of Leland's hand, and set the teacup on a metal box. He took up his shovel and rammed it into the coal bin again, then tossed another load into the firebox. Examining another gage, he leaned back against the wall.

"Like the shipping baron Franz Niva?" Cobain asked.

"He's my father. I hope he's okay," Leland said.

"Well, sonny boy, your name might be mud if those Burkers catch up with you. They seemed to have come to town to stay, and I don't think they're too picky as to who they kill."

"I guess so," Leland said. "I just wish I knew he was alright."

"Another twenty miles down the track is a midway-station with a note-gram wire. I need to stop there to take on some water. You can send him a message."

Leland's heart lifted. "That would be great."

"Provided we don't get shot at," Cobain added.

The steam wheel came to a halt along a single platform that ran the length of four wooden buildings. Leland and Cobain got off while Ella, Tommy, and the others looked from a passenger car window. Golden rays of sunlight were just peaking over the treetops as the two men looked in the long plate-glass window of the ticket station service office. Leland knocked. No answer was forth coming.

"Where ya at, ye old wretch?" shouted Cobain.

From down the platform the sound of hobnail boots on wood tapped out someone approaching. Leland and Cobain looked to see a bent old man in blue coveralls.

He looked up, shook his head, and pulled his pocket watch out of his vest pocket. He examined it for a moment, then closed it and replaced it.

"You're one day and five hours early. Did they change the schedule?" he asked.

"No, you old fool. Tiquan is under attack by the Burkmuran army and navy. They got the skies sealed off and probably the seas blockaded too," Cobain said.

The old man stopped just in front of his office, fished out some keys and opened the door.

"With all that, I guess you'd better come on in and wait while I fix a cup of bitter-bean brew."

He went to a shelf and took down a large metal can. Opening it, he scooped out the black powder into a metal pot and set the pot on a gas heater.

"Should be ready in a few minutes," the man said. "Now, what's all this about an attack?"

"Just look at your note-gram," Cobain barked.

The old man walked around a counter to a metal contraption with a graphite stylus clamped into its arm. He looked down at a piece of yellow paper that contained some writing.

"I'll be damned. Looks like we're at war," he said.

"What in Height's Hell have I been telling ya?"

"Okay son, don't lose yer balance." He sat down on the rickety wooden chair and opened a drawer. Taking out a bottle he pulled the cork and took a drink. "Have a nip, lads, it'll help us all think about what this means." He handed the bottle to Cobain. "If we're at war, what are ya doing here cozying up to me?"

Cobain took a long pull from the bottle then handed it to Leland.

"You old crock, me and this young fellow here barely made it out of Tiquan alive with bombs exploding all around and short-sighted soldiers trying to pot-shot us." He looked out the window at the steam-wheel and the others looking back at him. "This man here is Leland Niva, and he's got to send a note-gram to his father. Can you help?"

The old man tapped a name plate sitting on the desk that read *Richard Mulligan Bloodred, Chief Station Attendant.* "I can do what I bloody well like," he said. He took up a stylus and pad. "Where's the note going and what do you want it to say?"

Leland exhaled. "It's going to Burly Wood Station."

Richard wrote it down then looked at Leland expectantly.

Leland shook his head. "Perhaps I should write it myself?"

Richard stood and walked to a panel with holes in it. "You can do that," he said. He pulled up a wire from the table and plugged it into one of the holes on the panel. "Sit at the stylus table and write your note." He cranked a handle and a red light came on. "When the green light comes on, start writing your message."

They sat around waiting, but the light did

not change.

"Could they be out for some reason?" Leland asked.

Richard looked at the clock on the wall. "Not likely at this time of day. The wire has to be manned during business hours. I'll try the loop-back ringer." He stood up and walked to a wooden box on a table, cranked a handle a few times and waited. Nothing happened.

"Those Burkers must have cut the lines. That'll make quite a mess when we have to repair them." He sat back down and took a pull from the bottle.

"I need to fill the boiler with some water Rich. After that it'll take me twenty minutes to heat her back up, then we'll be on our way up to Jutland. If those Burkers are coming this way, you'd better come with us," Cobain said.

"And leave my post? I don't think so. Those Burkers can travel a rail into Height's Hell for all I care. Anyway, what kind of threat can one old man pose to them? If they come they'll most likely leave me be."

"I don't think so, Rich," Cobain said. "They came to Tiquan and started dropping bombs all over the city. They were killing women and children as they went; not just soldiers."

"Don't worry, lad, they'll be no threat to me," Richard added with a smile.

"I hope you're right. If not, this might be a last good bye." Cobain poked out his hand. The old man shook it then took another drink.

Cobain stood and left the room. He walked

down the platform to the steam-wheel and took hold of a long wrought iron chain that hung down from a water tower and pulled the spout over to the boiler. He climbed up into the pilothouse and flipped a switch to release the steam from the side valves. The air around the boiler filled with a thick white mist.

Leland stood up and shrugged his shoulders. "I guess I'll help Cobain," he said.

Richard nodded his head. "This is a strange time, son," he said. "There ain't much one man can do except his best."

Leland walked to the door, stopped, and looked back. "Do you think Hurgray has a chance?"

Richard chuckled. "We've never faced such a challenge before. It's anyone's guess at this point. We're a feisty breed. Those Burkers will pay in blood before it's done, I'm sure. When you get to Jutland look up my friend Carl Burmore. He has a civilian airship that he uses for trade and… business. Tell him I sent you."

"Where do we find him?"

"He has a warehouse by the Commerce District. Tell him Richard Bloodred sent you, he'll be receptive." Richard chuckled.

Leland nodded, then exited the office. Tommy shouted from the car.

"Hey, did you get through?"

"No. Looks like the Burkers cut the lines."

"You owe me ten forkels," Geris shouted from behind Tommy.

"What are we going to do?" Tommy asked.

"Head down the track to Jutland. There's a

man who might be able to help us."

Ella pushed her head out a window. "Who is he?"

"His name is Carl Burmore, and he may have an airship."

"May?" Tommy said.

Leland walked to the car. "Hopefully we can skirt the mountains toward Helsink."

"If we can get word to the governor there, he can mobilize the Phol army and navy," Tommy added.

"I just hope we make it."

Chapter 5

*Report to High Command: Boarded airship
456 and heading east toward Jutland. Estimated
time of arrival 1820 hours. Have confirmation from
Force Gail Seven Three that they can provide
convergence at Jutland to assist. End Report.*

***

They were approaching the outskirts of
Jutland. Cobain slowed the steam-wheel. The clack
of the rails slowed, and Leland exited the pilot
house. He maneuvered along the catwalk to the first
car and entered. Ella was sitting there reading a
book, a plate sat on the cocktail table, and the
remains of a cooked helios bird and a yam were
splayed out.

"I see you've eaten," Leland said.

Ella looked over at him and smiled. "There's
two plates in the galley; one for you and one for
Cobain. Why have we slowed?"

"We're entering the outskirts of Jutland.
Cobain thinks we'll be in the station in twenty
minutes."

Ella stood up and stretched her arms to the
ceiling. "Does Cobain know this Carl Burmore?"

"He doesn't, but he knows where his
warehouse is. The plan is that Tommy and I will
jump off as we pass and make contact, and see if
he'll help us," Leland said. "You, Geris, Crystal,
and Genya will stay onboard until the station." He
started to walk toward the galley. "I'd better take

Cobain some lunch; he's been mighty kind to us."

Leland walked through the connecting door, through another car, and to the dining station. There he found two plates covered with napkins. He took one plate and a bundle of silverware, and headed back toward the engine.

A few minutes later, the cars shuddered as the speed of the vehicle slowed again. Leland walked past Ella, stopped, then looked thoughtful. "Where's Tommy and the others?"

Ella chuckled. "They went forward to the observation car. Who knows what they're doing up there?" She gave him a cagy smile.

"I'll be back soon, and we can find out exactly what they're up to." He shook his head and laughed as he headed toward the pilothouse.

Ella felt an excitement at the thought of being alone with Leland. It was a feeling that tingled in her belly, and radiated throughout her body. She sat back down, took up her book, and crossed her legs. "Don't keep me waiting, Mr. Niva," she added in a sultry voice.

He looked surprised at her candor. "I'll be back faster than a messenger with a note-gram," he said and exited the car.

Leland entered the steam-wheel pilothouse. Cobain was sitting on the barrel with a teacup in his hand. "Care for a spot?"

"No thanks. I just came by to bring you lunch." Leland handed the plate and cutlery to Cobain. "How far to the warehouse?"

"Not far now. I slowed the old-girl down to

thirty miles per hour, and I'll slow her down to less than twenty in," he checked his watch, "thirteen more minutes." Cobain uncovered the plate and began to eat. "I want to say thanks for bringing me food and tea."

"I want to thank you for slowing down and picking us up," Leland said. "If you hadn't, we'd be in the clutches of those Burkers in Tiquan now. Who knows what they would have done with us?"

"True. They're not known for compassion or civility. I've heard that the Burker government lusts for our Augerland metals and wood," Cobain added.

"The evidence is clear – since they're here and plundering," Leland responded. "How will we know when to jump off?"

Cobain smiled. "I'll blow the whistle– two short blasts." He examined a gauge, flicked it once with his finger, then sat back. "I've heard Burmore's warehouse is about two miles from the station. The building is made of brick, and on the street a shingle hangs with an airship painted on it. I'm told that if you look at the side wall there's a faded mural that looks like a skull with two swords across it. Don't worry about your friends, I'll bring them safely in and get 'em situated at the Harland Inn just off Main Street. You won't be able to miss it. Now, you'd better go see to your friends before you have to jump."

Leland put out his hand and Cobain shook it.

"I hope we'll see each other again," Leland said.

"Hopefully at the inn and not in some Burker's prison camp." Cobain leaned forward and turned a valve and pulled on a long black lever. The steam-wheel slowed again. "It'll take some time for the roundhouse attendants to turn the rig around. Don't worry lad, if those Burkers come out here, they'll be in for a fight." He smiled. "Those who live out here, they don't mind scrapping one bit. Now, be off with ya, or you'll miss your mark."

Leland turned and left the pilothouse, went down the catwalk, and entered the car. Ella stood up and walked over to him. She took his hand in hers and looked up into his blue eyes with just the hint of a gentle smile.

"Don't say anything," Ella said, as she lifted her face up to his.

Leland wrapped his arm around her waist and pulled her in. He breathed in the air about her filling his lungs with her essence. His lips lay upon hers like a silk pillow against silk sheets.

Ella trembled beneath the weight of his passion as fire bore through her. She closed her eyes and all of the horror of the day before vanished.

For a moment the rhythmic clack of the wheels faded, and in the silence she felt his heart beating strongly against her breast. They broke the seal of their lips, and she inhaled deeply.

Ella blinked up at him, then stepped back. She exhaled, then with a look of command stated, "Now that we got that out of the way, let's take a look at what the others are finding so fascinating," She pulled him forward by the hand.

The connector door came open, and Leland stepped into the observation car. It was long with a glass ceiling and walls. Lounge chairs and squat wooden tables were positioned down the middle. A high-pitched whistling caught Ella's attention, and she pointed.

"Look, bullet holes," she said.

Leland saw the damaged panes of glass. He walked toward one, when Tommy waved at him.

"Down here." Tommy smiled broadly. Both Genya and Crystal were by him.

Taking Ella by the hand, Leland walked down to where Geris, Crystal, Genya, and Tommy were. Out the window green rolling hills passed.

He'd read about the Carper Expanse where the early settlers carved homes from within the tall rolling hills. Whole towns were made like that, and most were still occupied with simple farming families.

"I saw a painting of the Bruberry Street Theater in Vixenville once," Leland said while staring out the window. "The street lamps were all aglow, the paths were crowded with walkers, and all around were the dark green hills. I used to dream about visiting there, but my father said they were just colloquial remnants of a bygone age."

Leland looked forward out the metal and glass cone-shaped front of the car. A marker-sign passed. "The town of Jutland is just ahead. Cobain is going to signal us so we can jump off," he said to Tommy.

"Jump on, jump off, this is all becoming intolerable," Tommy said.

"Don't bellyache too much," Leland began, "or you'll upset your landing."

Tommy shook his head, then smiled. "What so inspires the gods, so inspires me," he said.

Leland grew somber and turned to Ella. "I don't know what the future has to offer us, but I like to think we've been put together for a reason. Even your brother Geris has a part to play, I'd wager."

"Sentimentality is overrated, Leland. All it gets a man is a broken heart and lost years," Geris said with a shake of his head.

Crystal and Genya stood up on either side of Tommy. The ladies took him by the arms. He grinned and Leland laughed. Geris scowled, and Ella shook her head.

"I expect to see you in Jutland," Crystal said to Tommy, then looked at Leland. "Don't let anything happen to my little Tommy," she added with just a hint of menace.

"Little?" Tommy said surprised.

"Not little in the right places," Genya said as her cheeks blushed red.

"Nonsense!" Geris blurted.

Two distinct blasts from the train whistle cracked the air. Tommy and Leland approached the side door. Buildings sped by on either side of the tracks— mostly large warehouses, some churning out black smoke from tall red-brick stacks.

"Okay," said Leland as he opened the external door. A column of air hit them as did the noise of the wheels on tracks.

"Jump!"

***

Hitting the ground, Leland's legs buckled and he rolled over the rough and knobby black and

71

white gravel that covered the edges of the tracks. .
Tommy did the same and they both got to their feet,
and brushed off the white dust and weeds from their
clothes.

As the train pulled away Leland saw Ella,
Genya, and Crystal standing there watching from
the doorway with fear written on their faces.

"Now where?" Tommy asked.

"We're looking for a warehouse that has a
skull painted on the side, or something like that,"
Leland said.

"Oh, that's lovely! A skull or something like
it," Tommy mocked.

"If you have a better idea, I'm all ears."

"No, I'm all in as you know. I hope this
fellow can get us to one of the Phol States," Tommy
said.

"Come on." Leland began crossing the many
tracks that led to various stone and brick buildings.

They walked for some time. Most of the
buildings seemed abandoned, the doors and
windows shuttered closed by heavy iron plates.
Turning down a paved street Leland noticed a dirty
stone marker. Next to it was a wooden pole with a
carved sign that read *Commerce Street.*

"Down here somewhere I think…"

Tommy stopped and pointed upward.
"Could it be here?"

On the side wall of the next building was the
outline of a faded skull against the redbrick.

Leland shrugged. "This must be it. Easy…
right?"

They approached a set of double doors that

faced the street. Leland rapped on it with his fist.

"Who is it?" a voice said from beyond the portals.

"My name is Leland, and my friend Tommy is with me. We were sent by Richard Bloodred. He said you might be able to help us."

"Bloodred? I knew a Richard Bloodred once." There were a few moments of silence, then the sound of metal unlatching from the other side was heard. One of the double doors opened. "You'd better come in." Only blackness waited beyond. "Well, don't stand there like a stunned horc, get in here."

Leland looked back at Tommy, then he took a breath and stepped into the darkness. Tommy followed.

The smell of dust and grease filled the air, and the sound of a machine churning in the darkness could be heard.

A ball of yellow-orange hovered in the darkness, and a face and a hand were visible. As their eyes adjusted, a tall slender man with muscular arms appeared. He looked down at Leland with penetrating eyes.

"Well, what is it?" the man asked.

"We're in a bit of a jam," Leland began.

"Jam? What sort of Jam?"

"I'd like to speak to Mister Burmore if you please," said Leland.

"I'm he, now out with it before I give you the dirty part of my boot," Burmore said.

"I suppose you've heard that Tiquan has fallen to Burkermuran?"

Burmore narrowed his gaze. "It came across over the note-gram last night. In fact the Burkers are coming down from the north even as we speak with an army and armored wheelers. I'm getting the blazes out of here, and you should too, if you know what's good for you."

Leland nodded. "That's why we're here. There are six of us, and we need to get to Phol as soon as possible. I'm Leland Niva, and my father—"

"I know the name well," Burmore said. "So, you're Franz Niva's son? I'll be damned." He took a few steps back and pulled a chair from the darkness and sat. "Did Richard know this?"

Leland nodded.

"He sent you here for my help? That old bastard sure has a sense of humor." Burmore chuckled but didn't look amused. "No doubt he told you that I'm no friend of the Phol Empire. In fact I fought against them when they invaded the Highland Territories."

"I'm sorry for that," Leland said. "But now we need your help to get away from the Burkers. Those blue uninformed bastards are on their way here, and their minds are filled with evil. I can pay you once we get to Phol, but all I have now is a few forkels."

Burmore looked down at his boots for a moment. "Money?" He stood up. "Where are you running from?"

"Tiquan. It was under heavy bombardment when we snagged a ride on a passing steam-wheel. We narrowly escaped," Leland said.

Tommy cut in. "Ya, the soldiers were nearly on us. We were lucky that Cobain slowed to let us on."

"Cobain? The steam-wheel pilot? He helped you? He told you how to find my warehouse?" Burmore's face took on an angry expression.

"He did," Leland said.

Burmore's features softened, then he lifted the lantern. "Well, I suppose I can't blame him under the circumstances. You'd better follow me." As he walked he looked back over his shoulder. "While I don't like the Phol Empire, I really despise Burkmuran."

They walked through the warehouse.

Tommy's curiosity was peaked. "Really, why do you hate the Burkers?"

"That's my business," Burmore said, then grunted as he started up some wooden stairs along the far wall.

Leland and Tommy followed. Tommy made it to the middle of the stairs as the whole staircase creaked loudly and shifted slightly. He looked back into the dark at Leland whose face was colored in the dull orange hue of Burmore's lantern. Leland nodded his head forward, and they both continued up.

"Dangerous stairs," Tommy said.

"They serve their purpose," Burmore added, as he reached a dirty wooden door and opened it. "Come on in and let's see what we can work out."

Leland and Tommy stepped in. It was a room with no windows. Burmore hung the lantern on a hook. He sat at a makeshift desk and pulled out some maps.

"The Burkers are coming down from the Pi inlet along the coast here." Burmore pointed. "And, if we say they're traveling at top speed, they'll get here by late tonight, or tomorrow morning." He inhaled deeply then exhaled.

"Damn, I hate to be driven out of another place where I've become comfortable." Looking up at Tommy and Leland he appeared to take stock of them. "Okay, I'll help you get clear of here. But we do it my way. The first moment I have any argument out of you, you're over the side – get me?"

Tommy's voice cracked. "Over the side?"

"He means he'll put us off the airship," Leland added.

"Correct," said Burmore. "Now, have a look at these charts." He pointed along a lateral line. "This is the air-canal northern gale. It blows at five thousand feet and can take us to Penning Row in twenty hours. I'll need your help to load the ship and get her ready."

"We'll do whatever we can to help," Leland affirmed.

"Good. Now, follow me and we can get this circus on the road." Burmore folded his charts and put them into a leather bag that hung from a leather strap at his side. "Each of you can only take," he paused and thought, "Twenty pounds."

"All we have is what's on our backs," Tommy said.

Burmore smiled. "Well then, that makes it easy."

Chapter 6

Report to High Command: Steam-wheel that escaped Tiquan found in Jutland. Assault on Jutland in progress. Fighting is house to house. Niva and Garland children are not accounted for. Airship Ocronis reports a lifter visible near west end of the town. Military and Suspol moving to interdict. End report.

***

Leland watched the western sky from the porch of the Harland Inn. Burmore was inside instructing the others on what they could and couldn't do on the airship. The sun appeared as a massive ball of glowing blood while it melted beyond the horizon. A hand fell on his shoulder and he jumped.

"Height's Hell," Leland said.

"It's beautiful," Ella stated as she came alongside him. She took his hand in hers and shivered with the cold air. "I don't like being high up," she added.

He put his arm around her. "Not much choice at the moment. Don't worry, I'll be there with you."

They stood there for a moment when Burmore spoke up.

"We need to get going. Town Guard-Scouts have reported the Burker infantry have entered the city. They're less than five miles from here. They've set fire to some of the town's outer buildings along the way." He gestured toward a set of steps that led to the driveway and road. "We'll be better off in the air."

Burmore led the way to the street and away from the inn.

All six of them followed Burmore as he wove his way along the street. They walked for some time, as the ghostly orange glow from the north grew brighter.

In the middle of a street, Burmore slammed the shutter down on the lantern and motioned for them to get into an alley. A host of men with rifles rushed by. Even in the darkness Leland saw they were Burker soldiers. Two men in trench coats followed, both holding pistols.

Burmore watched as they approached his warehouse. One of the soldiers shot away the lock and slid open the door. Soldiers went in. A few moments later two came out.

"We have to move fast," Burmore said and led them through the alley and dark streets.

After many twists and turns, they arrived at a deserted amphitheater. The building appeared abandoned.

"In here," Burmore said, as he pulled aside a false wall to reveal a long, dark hallway. He stepped in. "Close the passage behind you," he added over his shoulder.

A strong smell of mildew and mold filled the air. The sound of dripping echoed down the hall. They walked for a minute, then found themselves in an oblong field two hundred yards long.

In the middle of the field sat an eighty foot

long airship gondola, and a two hundred foot long balloon hovering above it. At the stem and stern were amber lanterns illuminating the area.

"Wow," Crystal murmured, as she stepped out onto the field.

"We helped get it ready," Tommy proudly stated.

Genya giggled. "You're a handy fellow, Tommy Wayne!"

They marched over to where a plank led up to a hatch in the side. One by one they entered the gondola.

"It looks like a sailing ship," Geris said.

"I had it made out of iron-reed rattan," Burmore told the assembled.

"Isn't that the reeds that grow somewhere near Piptian on the other side of the desert?" Ella asked.

Burmore hung his lantern from the lower deck ceiling and opened the shutter.

"That's right. I've done some trading with the Velenar who trade with the Piptianians. I sent my design, and they sent this back ." He motioned with his hand to the hull and pointed at the opening. "Close that door if you don't mind."

Leland pulled the door shut and rotated a brass bar down to secure it to the frame.

"The Desert Ghosts," Geris whispered.

"Yes, the Desert Ghosts," Burmore said.

"I've never heard of an airship gondola being made from this kind of reed before. I've heard of houses having it for a roof, but not an airship," Genya added.

"Those engineers in Piptian did a splendid job; light, rugged, and fire resistant. One can't ask for much more in an airship." Burmore smiled and pointed toward the back. "There are three sets of sleeping cabins back there. Below is the cargo area, and forward is the observation post. Up on deck sits the steam generator and other components that make up my ship. Try not to mess with anything, and if you have any doubt about something, ask me before touching."

A crashing sound echoed in the arena. The distinctive breaking of wood filled the air. The sound of boots smashing against the ground came from one of the long halls that led from the field into the bleachers.

Burmore pulled on a handle and a door opened above him. A ladder dropped to his feet and he began climbing up. "Prepare to detach the mooring lines," he called back.

Orders were being shouted from the darkness, then the glow of lanterns appeared halfway up along a row of seats. Dark figures were swarming into the bleachers, the lanterns rocking back and forth as the men ran toward the fleeing fugitives.

The airship broke loose from the ground and rocked from side to side as it quickly rose into the night air. It took a few moments before stabilizing, then was still.

"Halt – that ship is now the property of the Burkmuran army!" shouted a man's voice below.

The sound of popping filled the air as someone yelled, "Cease fire you idiots! You'll hit the kids!"

"Come up on deck, there is something you should see," Burmore called down as the ship continued to rise.

Ella climbed up first, followed by her girlfriends and Geris. Leland and Tommy brought up the rear. Sturdy rigging secured the gondola to three balloons that made up the lifters.

At the aft was a forecastle with a room below, fitted with lead panes of glass. Burmore was atop steering a large wheel. A curved staircase on the right side wound up to the wheel-deck, and on the left hung a lantern. In the middle of the decking was a ten-foot-long metal cylinder, three feet wide standing on six legs.

Burmore secured the wheel and came down. He approached the cylinder and opened a hatch at the back, and put in a lump of coal. He adjusted several valves and observed half a dozen gages. "Take a look over the larboard side," he said.

Ella saw in the distance an airship on the ground. "What is it doing there?"

"The real question is, why did an advance complement of the Burkers show up at my lifter site?" Burmore asked.

"The voice of the man that shouted from down there... I've heard him before," Leland said. "He tried to kidnap Ella and her friends in Tiquan a few days ago."

"So, why is he here now?" Burmore opened the boiler door and tossed in more fuel.

"They're after me," Ella said. "Or, Crystal, or Genya... or maybe all of us."

"They are eager to bring us down," Burmore added. "Don't worry. Even if they shoot a few holes into my lifters, we'll get clear of them. That's a nice thing about my ship, easy to repair." He adjusted a few valves and looked at some gages again. "I wonder why they're after the lot of you."

"I don't know," Leland added.

Geris came over. "How does this contraption work?"

Burmore smiled at the question. "The water is heated in the steam generator and flows along those tubes." He pointed up toward the balloons. "The heat is fed into my lifters, then the water is recycled and passes through radiators that are suspended in the wings on either side. The force of the hot water moving in one direction pulls the cold water back into the tank. I can keep heating my balloon for days without landing, provided I have enough fuel... food, and drink."

"I hear the Burkers use hydrogen to lift their air cruisers," Geris said.

"Expensive, and it's complex to make that gas. Not to mention the gas escapes after a while. All I have to do is land and load up on coal or wood... or dung for that matter, then I'm off again." He chuckled, opened the fire hatch, and tossed in a few more chunks of coal.

Ella looked over the rattan railing. "How high can you get in this thing?"

"I've been as high as twenty thousand feet once. I passed out and when I came too, I was blue with cold and had landed near Yental Junction along the Killiman Mountains. I've found that ten thousand feet is an adequate height when I'm moving cargo." He looked around at his passengers. "I think on this trip, though, we'll only be flying at five thousand feet."

"What happens if the ship is shot down?" Crystal asked.

"Not to worry; I have escape sails. If we're going to crash, and you can get to the railing here," he pointed at canvas straps with buckles, "loop these around your shoulders and these loops around your legs and just leap off. The sail will open automatically, and you'll float like a feather down to the ground. If you're in the hold, there are two there – one fore and one aft. Just put on the harness, open the hatch near the keel and drop out."

"Drop out," Genya said. "You must be joking?"

"Not at all." Burmore realized that the six were looking at him as if he'd gone mad.

"It's quite safe... unless you land in the water, some trees, or the desert. At least you'll have a sporting chance; much better than just plummeting. I had to do it once during the Highland War. I landed in a damned roark field. When I woke, I had a half dozen of those hairless roarks snorting around me, licking my face. I must have looked like a child's lollypop!" He chuckled.

"That's not encouraging," Geris added.

"Let's hope we don't have to do that," Tommy said.

"Most likely not," Burmore replied. He pointed at areas around the deck where the rattan was woven into seats. "Have a sit and watch the world go by." He turned a valve, and pulled a polished brass lever. The ship moved forward and began to pick up speed. He then went aft and up on the forecastle.

"That Burker airship is lifting off," he said and went to the lanterns and put out the lights. "We'll need to run dark for tonight. Now, you'd better get some rest, you all look spent."

"That's an understatement," said Crystal.

***

Leland felt like he was falling, then woke with a start. He looked around in the darkness and realized he was in the airship hold. Getting to his feet, he went up on deck.

The deck was illuminated in the faint glow of starlight. He heard a rustling sound on the forecastle, and went up the stairs. Burmore looked over, acknowledged his presence, and then focused on the navigational compass.

The airship captain turned a brass bezel, then adjusted the ship's wheel.

"I don't often have company on my trips," Burmore said.

"You don't take passengers?" Leland asked.

"Not the kind that help me with the ship."

Leland walked over to the aft railing and looked down. Three propellers were turning, and directional fins were pointed to the one side. The ship was making a wide turn. He looked up at the stars.

"Looks like we're heading east?" Leland

stated.

Burmore unrolled a small map over the compass. Lines on the map glowed dark blue. He measured between two points with calipers, then looked thoughtful for a moment and checked his pocket watch.

"Fifteen hours to Penning Row as long as we keep at five thousand feet." He adjusted the wheel again and tied it off. "The Northern Gale will keep us on course from here on out," he said "I think we've given those Burkers the slip. I did a few maneuvers not long after you all went to sleep. Their forward lanterns were heading straight south and was five hundred feet below us, last I saw."

Burmore walked to the stairs, went down onto the main deck. He adjusted some valves at the steam generator. "Come on and have a sit," he told Leland.

Leland obliged. He looked out over the port side and saw the outline of the mountains in the dim starlight. Burmore pulled the cork from a bottle, took a drink and handed it to Leland.

"It sure is getting cold up here," Leland said with a shiver.

Burmore nodded, stood and went to a rigging cabinet. He pulled out two gray pea coats and came back, "Here, put this on. It's going to get much colder as the night wears on. Your friends won't notice, as I've set the hot water circulators to keep the gondola warm."

Leland took another drink. "How long have you been flying?"

"Let me see," Burmore took back the bottle.

"Something like twenty years now. I was recruited to fly in the Highland Air Corps. When your country invaded mine I was pressed into service. It was a messy business. Airships blasting away at each other with peroxide cannons - men burned by that harsh chemical when shells crashed into them, while others fell from gondolas to their deaths.

"There were twenty of us to a crew; two men per repeating ballistae, and four men to every cannon. I did all the navigating, and was responsible for lifting off and landed." He took a drink and leaned his back against the railing. "They say that once you've flown, it gets into your blood and you crave to be in the air all the time. That's certainly the case with me."

"What happened after the war?" Leland asked.

"The whole business could hardly really be called a war. It lasted three months. Our air corps was lost in the first month. We were hopelessly out numbered and out gunned. Nonetheless, afterward, I escaped to the north east. For a time I did some prospecting along the border of the Rema Desert. Have you ever heard of tapping holes?"

"No." Leland shook his head.

"They're places where the hard rock of the desert has collapsed and formed a water-filled cistern. Me and a friend, Jack Parker, took up looking for gold in those subterranean caverns."

"Did you find any?"

"We found more than we bargained for." Burmore took a drink and handed the bottle to Leland. "We were as far into the Rema as one can get and not die from the heat."

Burmore got up and checked the boiler, then returned.

"One day while we were exploring uncharted tapping holes, we came across a tunnel. It was cut with precision into the rock. It looked like some miners had beaten us there. We lit our lanterns and entered to have a look around.

"After about twenty minutes, we saw a light at the far end." He became lost in his thoughts. "Our lantern could only illuminate a few feet in front of us, but as we got closer to that strange light we became aware it was moving... hovering... like an small airship.

"At an arched doorway we entered a cavern. I was awe struck. Piles of gold nuggets were everywhere as if carelessly piled into this chamber. The strange hovering light came toward us. I can remember the exact words it spoke to this day— *chi co mo*, it said."

He put his feet up on another wicker chair and leaned back against the railing again.

"I dropped the lantern, but luckily it didn't shatter. 'Chi co mo', it said again. I scooped up the lantern. Jack was already at a dead run in front of me. That light came after us... a ghostly, horrible thing that pursued us down the tunnel. I saw the brightness overpowering our lantern light.

"When we arrived at the tapping hole we scrambled up the rope ladder we'd used to get into it. The sun was directly overhead and the sunlight was streaming in. Halfway up, I slipped. The lantern and I fell forty feet into the pool of water below. The cold water washed over me and I struggled to get to the surface. That's when I saw it in the murky depths. There was a glimmer around the edges of the pool. Gold coins, by the hundreds."

"What of that strange light?" Leland said.

"To tell the truth, at that point I forgot about it completely. I broke the surface, took a breath and went back down. When I came up again, I had a fist full of twenty-forkel coins. I called to Jack who was watching me from the tapping hole rim. He sent down a bucket on a rope and we hauled up several buckets full of coins."

"Is that how you bought this airship?"

"I put the money to good use," Burmore said as he looked out to port. "Poor Jack didn't make it out of the desert though."

"What happened?"

"As we were making our way out of the desert, we saw a caravan of Velenar. We'd heard the legends that they ate the flesh of settlers, and did vile and terrifying things to those they captured. We reasoned that was how the coins came to be in the tapping hole in the first place. Some lost group of settlers, hid their money from the desert ghosts, then were murdered by those white terrors. So we fled into the desert."

Burmore buttoned up his coat to his neck then took a swig from the bottle.

"The heat was tremendous out there, and it was more than ten hours until sunset. Our water didn't last long; we knew we couldn't get to another hole. In our haste we became disoriented in the dunes."

"Didn't you have one of those giant lizards to carry your stuff?" Leland asked, now engrossed in the story.

Burmore took another swig and handed the bottle back to Leland.

"No, we were just scouting out sites - better on foot to keep those claim-hackers off our tracks." The sky captain looked up. "Jack fell just before the sun set; he couldn't go on. The buckets were our downfall; slowing our pace, and sapping our strength. It had to be a hundred and forty degrees in the shade. I gave him the last of my water, but he died soon after. At least I made his last moments a little better."

Burmore looked out over the railing for a moment, then back at Leland. His face had taken on a sad expression. He drew in a deep breath.

"I knew I'd not be too far behind ole Jack. There was no way I'd ever get out of that place alive. It must have been delirium that over took me because I began to sing loudly, as if singing to the gods."

He stood up and took back the bottle, downed two gulps, then began singing.

"Here on the Mier rising; here on the Mier son; go heft the forkle darling; carry loaded righteous gun. Burn yer dowry, burn the farm, and leave old Ma behind. Take up rifle and your gun, and save the Highlands one last time!"

He looked at Leland and smiled. "I figured it was over for me. My head was splitting with pain, and I was driving hard down that black tunnel to death."

Ella appeared and came close.

Leland looked over at her. "I was just listening to Burmore about his adventures."

"I'm sorry for interrupting," Ella said. "Please, Mister Burmore, go on." She rubbed her arms and shivered. "It's terribly cold out here," she said.

Leland opened his coat. "This old coat can fit two," he told her.

Ella squeezed in with him as best she could. He enclosed her with his arms.

Even in the darkness, Burmor's smile was visible. He cleared his throat and continued with his story.

"I don't know how long I'd been out... a day, a week...it could have been years. But after a time I came too. My skull was still aching and I felt strong hands... giant hands, lifting me up to a sitting position. A bowl was put to my lips, and I drank. It was more wonderful than smoking blissroot, or taking a dose of liar's lark. The pain was gone, and I realized I was on green grass next to a rushing, vibrant brook. A large white face was looking down at me with kind eyes. I didn't understand what it was trying to tell me. Another appeared, and yet another. I realized they were Velenar and all hope of surviving vanished from my heart."

"But you're here to tell the tale," Ella observed.

"Right you are, my lovely young lady. You see, the Velenar are pacifists. They don't eat flesh of any kind. They wouldn't dream of harming any

living thing, and in fact, they saved my life.
Surprisingly, they also saved all the gold too."

"Why?" Leland asked.

"That's an even longer story." He took out
his watch and looked at it. "You'd both better get
some sleep. I'll wake everyone at first light."

"What about you?" Ella asked with concern.

Burmore chuckled. "Me? I'll take a few
naps, that's all I need. There's little for us to hit up
here, and I've fixed the wheel on course. Sleep well,
there's nothing to fear."

Ella took Leland by the hand. "Come on,
you heard the captain. I have something to show
you down below," she said.

Leland stood, looked back at Burmore, then
followed her down into the lower deck. Burmore
was right; there was a significant difference in
temperature from the top to the bottom. Instantly he
began sweating under the thick wool coat. He took
it off and hung it on a peg by the ladder.

Ella led him to the observation room at the
bow, and they looked out the windows into the
darkness.

"The darkness – it seems to just swallow up
all the war and violence," Ella said.

Leland put his arm around her. "We'll get
through this. Your parents will be okay. No Burker
would dare harm Emerald Garland and invoke the
wrath of Ciciro."

"Maybe so…" Ella's voice trailed off.

Next to her was a platform with a mattress
on it. She lay down on it and motioned for Leland to
lie beside her. He did. She snuggled in close and

placed her head on his chest.

       "I can hear your heart," she said.

       "And I can feel yours," Leland softly added.

He kissed her on the head, then closed his eyes.

Chapter 7

*Report to High Command: Intelligence
believes the targets are aboard rogue airship.
Intelligence further reports that the ship belongs to
a Mister Carl Burmore, known smuggler and
wanted by the Burkmuran authorities. Advise. End
report.*

***

Tommy pointed to port and downward.
"Another ship!"

Burmore climbed down from the forecastle
and looked. It was a Burkmuran airship not more
than a mile to their port side. The dawn was ready
to break, and the soft light of morning was
reflecting off the other ship's lifter skin.

"Looks like they're flashing a light at us,"
Tommy said.

Burmore read the signal. "Give us the
passengers and you can go free." Burmore laughed.
"How stupid do they think I am? There's no way
they'll let me leave – alive that is."

"Are you going to answer them?" Tommy
looked concerned.

"It's best that we don't. I wouldn't want to
encourage them."

Burmore went back up the stairs to the
wheel and laid out his map.

"I'm beginning to get the impression you're
all very valuable cargo," Burmore added.

"They're signaling again," Tommy pointed.

"They're just telling us that once they're in range, they'll fire on us," Burmore casually said.

"Fire on us?" Tommy looked pale.

"Don't worry. Look ahead and you'll see a pirate's answered prayers."

Tommy turned his gaze forward and saw a wall of thunderhead clouds backed up over the mountains. "How is that an answered prayer?"

"The best defense in an air battle is concealment," Burmore said.

"You're taking us in there?" Tommy's look became graver.

A flash of light illuminated the clouds. "And so the gods of Dale lit the way for Fallon, whom the searing lights did blaze his path to freedom," Burmore recited. "That's where we're going, so if you're a religious man I'd suggest you get right and proper chummy with one of the gods." He laughed. "Those Burkers would be mad to follow us in there."

"What does that make us?" Tommy asked.

"The answer is in the explanation," Burmore added as he unhooked the wheel and spun it. The ship came around twenty degrees and headed straight for the raging storm.

The airship entered the first thunderhead. Moisture immediately formed on all the outer surfaces. Flashes of light illuminated the mist followed by distant, but powerful, crack of thunder. Burmore stood at the wheel, adjusting the course, looked at his pocket watch, and observed the compass as he did.

Leland and Tommy stood on deck as the turbulence began to grow. The gondola shook several times, then a deafening crack of thunder caused the boiler to vibrate like a bell. Rain began to pelt them, then came the stinging hail. Burmore fought to keep the craft on course, as pebbles of ice piled up along the gondola edges.

He secured the wheel and Called to Leland. "Come up here, lad!

Leland came up and stood next to the captain.

"Look here," Burmore said, as he showed Leland a battery of controls. "Look to me for direction. I'll tell you what to do. Now watch me closely; this valve controls the steam to the propellers at the aft, and this one controls the heat to the lifters. This one allows the hull to be heated, and this one increases or decreases the recovery circulators. Do you understand?"

Leland nodded.

"Good, now stay sharp and keep ready."

The ship shook with violent winds. Burmore struggled to hold the wheel on course.

"Power to the lifters," Burmore shouted, "and decrease the prop speed by two turns."

The ship pitched slightly and turned in the dark mist. Burmore had his watch out as he held the wheel with one hand. He looked over at Leland. "Increase the circulator a turn, and open the prop to full... now!"

The craft tilted up at the bow a few degrees as the craft picked up speed.

"Open the valve to the lifters and add more

fuel to the fire."

"How do I add to the fire?" Leland tried to disguise his growing panic.

"Sorry lad – that lever to your side controls the coal auger. Pull it out an inch," Burmore said.

Leland moved quickly. He turned the handle on the lifter valve, then pulled the lever. A distinct clacking sound added to the storm sounds. The ship tilted to the side.

A cross wind was battering them. The clouds thinned, and Leland realized that they were between two jagged mountain peaks— the cliff walls not more than a hundred meters to either side. He glanced at Burmore, who was looking at his watch, then down at his compass.

"Tommy!"

Tommy moved from the riggers-cabinet where he was holding on. "Yes," he called back.

"Get up here and pull back on the bow plain lever – quickly! I have to hold the wheel precisely, or we'll be dashed to bits."

Tommy rushed up onto the forecastle. To Burmor's right was a large brass lever sticking up from the deck. He grabbed it but it didn't move.

"It's stuck or something," he shouted.

"The release is along the side of the lever. Pull it out, by God, pull it out and pull it back!" Burmore said.

Tommy found a metal pin and pulled it out, then pulled back on the device. The bow rose another few degrees. The gondola shook violently as the sound of crumbling rock was heard. The girls down below screamed; Leland was thrown to the deck, and Tommy to the side. The craft pitched forward as the balloons pulled the ship over rocks and into other unseen things in the mist, then it righted and rocked back and forth. Thunder cracked again and lightning flashed. Blue static danced across the metal surfaces of the boiler, as the odor of ozone filled the air. Hail smashed them for some time, then more lightning, and more thunder.

After a few minutes, the hail turned to a cold stinging rain. The ship kept moving as the tempo of the storm was slowing and fading to the aft. Burmore looked at his watch and seemed to be counting. A few minutes later he looked up.

"Leland, decrease the props, increase circulators." He looked to the side. "Tommy, push the lever to the middle position." Burmore put his watch back in his pocket and cranked the wheel to larboard. He examined the compass, and when he was satisfied, spun the wheel and secured it again.

"There, that wasn't so hard was it?" he asked.

Lightning flashed in the white mist. Rain pelted them as a strong wind pushed them from the port side. "Those Burkers won't get over that pass with that gigantic airship anytime soon. They'll have to go down to Harrow's Gate to get across, if they even figure out what we did." He laughed. "I think we're quite safe for now."

"Safe!" Geris said coming up onto the deck. "You almost bloody killed us and now you say we're safe?"

"The key word you said is *almost*. Besides, it's probably only six hundred feet down to the ground if you want to get off?" Burmore said with a wry smile.

Geris staggered to the base of the forecastle and looked up. "I'll take my chances with you, but for the record I think that was a reckless move."

"It was, but now those flyboys back there won't be dogging our heels." Burmore took out his watch and looked over at Leland. "Cut prop speed and lifters, and open the circulators full. No need for more fuel at the moment, *Mister Niva*," he said in a military manner. "You can close off the auger."

Leland did as he was instructed and the ship began to lose altitude. Tommy waited until he noticed Burmore grinning at him.

"You boys did a splendid job. I'd be proud to call you crew," Burmore said while watching his compass and altimeter. "We'll be out of the clouds soon and I'll need you,Tommy, to look for a wide clearing and a long red X on the ground. When you see it, call to me. Leland, we'll need some momentum at that point and I'll need you to open the prop speed two turns. When we land, you can all buy me a drink for saving your hides," he said with a hint of self-satisfaction.

They broke through the clouds and a pine forest came into view. The sun was blazing from the east. A sudden onset of heat and humidity hit them all. Below, the green rows of trees looked like spear tips. The vast forest extended for miles in every direction. At the far eastern side, a reddish plain and a distant white light dominated the landscape.

"What's that?" Tommy asked.

"That's the Rema Desert," Burmore said.

"But what's that light?" Geris pointed.

Burmore took off his wool coat and pulled a pair of dark blue spectacles from his pocket and put them on. "That, my curious friend, is the White Desert. No man's ever crossed it. It's the domain of the Velenar tribes. Somehow they survive in that hell. That tan-colored band you see is the perimeter. In that zone the temperatures can get up to a hundred and fifty degrees in summer, and it's many miles deep."

"How do the Velenar survive there?" Leland asked.

"Somehow they do. All I can tell you is that the desert is deadly."

"I've heard that the Desert Ghosts are like the Cargarian Apes who lurk in the jungle. Brutes if you ask me," Geris said.

"You couldn't be more wrong," Burmore told him. "But they are not human, though they look very much like humans."

"Monsters I've heard," Crystal said, as she came up onto the deck. "It was too hot down there, but now that I'm up here, it's pretty much the same." She loosened the laces on her dress to allow her cleavage to be exposed. "There, that's better."

Geris shook his head in disapproval.

"There are a lot of legends out there. Mostly fabrications by people who imagine more than is true," Burmore added.

Genya came up onto the deck, looked at Crystal, and quickly undid her own front laces.

"A small relief," Crystal said as she fanned her chest.

"But, they saved you once. Why did they do it?" Ella asked Burmore.

"All I can tell you is that when my brain was boiling under that brutal sun, I thought I was done for. When I woke in that green paradise, I was sure I'd died."

"How'd you get back," Leland asked.

Burmore chuckled. "They led me underground, into a dark cool tunnel. We walked for what seemed like days. We ate cave mushrooms and drank a strange blue liquid they brought. Finally, we came to a place where a shaft of light shone down, and a rope hung from a vertical hole. I climbed at least a hundred feet and emerged out an ancient well. They secured my buckets, and I hauled them up one at a time. Quickly I buried them, then sought help. Once I'd found civilization I purchased a morg and brought it back and picked up my wealth."

"Morg?" Genya asked.

"The giant lizards the settlers use to travel and farm with," Geris said.

"That sounds disgusting," Crystal blurted. "I've heard they are smelly and disagreeable."

Burmore chuckled. "You really should get out more and make your opinions on fact and not hearsay."

Crystal harrumphed, found one of the wicker seats, and sat down. Genya walked toward the bow.

Tommy shouted, "I see a red cross in the middle of a clearing three points to port!"

"Good lad," Burmore called back, then

turned the wheel. "Leland, turn the propellers two full turns."

The ship lurched forward. Below, the trees moved past, to the aft lightning flashed, and thunder crashed and boomed. In front, a wide green clearing with a large red X in the middle waited.

"Turn the lifter valve four turns and wait for my order to turn it off." He watched closely as they were descending. The hull clipped the tops of a few tall pines as it came within the green expanse.

"Four turns, Mister Niva,"

The ship leveled out.

Burmore held the wheel with one hand and reached over and pulled the lever with the other. The bow lifted up slightly.

"Lifter valve full off!"

The ship hit the ground and stayed. Burmore pulled a few small levers and rotated some valves, then went down onto the deck as the lifter balloons were deflating.

"Help me secure the lifters and put them into their cradles," Burmore said. "Then, let's get ashore."

In short order the balloons were stowed. Burmore went below where he opened the side hatch and extended the gangplank. "All out," he said.

The clearing was large, three hundred yards wide, and two hundred in length. The grass was dark green and thick. Down the middle of the clearing was a layer of red dust that formed a gigantic X.

Burmore strapped on a holster and put a pistol into it. Leading the way he walked onto the grass and toward a set of log cabins along the perimeter. The others followed closely behind.

When they were nearly halfway, a large, hairy, dark brown creature came toward them at a run.

"Height's Hell, what is that thing?" Genya cried out.

Tommy and Leland stepped in front of the girls. Geris hid behind Burmore.

"Stay here," Burmore ordered, and took off at a run shouting loudly and waving his arms as he did so.

Burmore collided with the hairy creature and was felled. The monster was on him, and he was rolled from side to side. Yelling and swearing echoed in the glade. Then, Burmore stood and leapt onto the beast, locking his arms around its massive neck. In the distance a man was approaching holding a long-rifle.

"Why doesn't he shoot?" cried Genya.

"That thing is going to kill him!" Crystal shouted.

The beast stood up, dwarfing Burmore by the height of three men, spread its arms wide, and roared. Burmore fell from its neck, ran in front of the monster, and shouted back. The beast roared again, then Burmore pointed his finger at the creature and shouted. "Bang!"

The monster fell on its back. Leland, Tommy, and Geris looked at each other.

"What just happened?" Leland asked.

102

Burmore walk over to the creature and appeared to hug it. The other man arrived, and the two shook hands. They talked for a moment, then Burmore pointed back at the assembled onlookers. He waved them over. "Come ahead!"

They approached the two men and the monster with some trepidation. Once near, it was clear the hairy beast was enormous. It stood up, dwarfing them all, and sat down with its hind legs out in front of it.

Burmore bowed to the beast. "Esteemed Hyroke, let me introduce my recent friends. This is Crystal, Genya, Ella, Geris, Tommy and Leland."

The creature shook its head and bellowed, then added several low growls.

Burmore turned to the man standing there. "David, these are some friends acting as my crew. I'd appreciate it if you'd treat them as family. Kids, this is David Harcrow, the sheriff and mayor of Kipper's Grove."

David looked them over with a smile. "I'd be honored to do so. Come to the kitchen and we'll all sit, have some food, and parley." He led the way toward the cabins, but over his shoulder he said, "Hyroke, ya coming? I've got honey and kippling grubs for ya, if yer staying."

The creature snorted, growled and then shook its head from side to side.

"Better things to do?" David asked. "Fine, be off with ya. Come next Queryday and I'll trade ya some grain for vemer roots."

The creature stood up and walked off into the forest.

Chapter 8

Report to High Command: Pilot of the enemy airship has steered vessel into cloudbank. Lost sight at 1025 hours. Moving to mountain passage at Harrow's Gate. End report.

***

Cabins were laid out in rows. Between the rows were streets paved with gray wooden planks. A reddish dust seemed to coat most things, and several streams came down from the mountains, and passed through the town.

David led them to a large four story cabin, and entered. After some platitudes and introductions, they were shown to the dining room. David sat at the opposite end of a long wooden table. From the kitchen came several women in matronly clothes carrying pots of soup and trays of vegetables. The food was placed along the table.

"We've not seen the likes of you, Carl Burmore, for quite some time. Been up to no good, I take it?"

Burmore scooped some dumplings from a pot and put them into his bowl. "Just trying to carve out a living like you folks."

"Trade has fallen off in the last few years since the platinum rush petered out. I'd say we see half as many ships now come over and around the mountain as we used to. What's the news from the cities?"

"War," Burmore stated. "Burkmuran has

invaded the mainland, and seem bent on taking over the whole of Augerland."

"Seems every time I see you, you're coming from, or going to a war." David shook his head. "But I guess we can't hold you accountable for that."

"Do you still have that hot springs bathhouse?" Burmore asked.

"It's in the same place as it's always been. So is Katrina."

Burmore looked uncomfortable. "Karina is still here?"

"She never left. Has the same trading post, same cabin, and same way about her," David said, then chuckled.

"Who's Katrina?" Geris asked.

Burmore looked over at Geris with a scowl, but said nothing. David gave a knowing smirk.

The host scooped food onto his plate, and his guests followed suit. The food was rich, salty, and often thick with gravy or sauce.

"I'd like to thank you, Mr. Harcrow, for your hospitality. By the way, where exactly are we?" Genya asked.

David looked at the assembled group, then at Burmore. "Crew, eh?"

"I said *acting as crew*. They were recommended to me by Bloodred. The Burkers want them for some reason; though I think I can guess why."

"Well, young lady, you've landed in Kipper's Grove, the last stop for anyone doing anything north along the platinum road. We're all pleased as pie to have you here." He smiled.

"What was that thing that attacked Burmore?" Geris asked.

"Thing?" David looked confused. "You don't mean old Hyroke, do you?"

"Yes."

"Hyroke is not a thing, but a him. None of you know about the forest folks?" He looked around the table. All were quiet. "Fifty six years ago when the first men came to this area, they found it occupied by the Redar peoples. Hyroke is one of them and he owns a hut-cave a quarter mile toward the desert lip. He and his people have inhabited these lands for thousands of years.

"He comes here to trade for goods on occasion. It takes some time to learn their customs and language. Ole Burmore speaks Redar fluently." David turned to Burmore. "I've sent word for you to have a cabin near the river— Farley's old place. He moved on a few years ago. I think he's living down at Harrow's Gate now; something to do with spider silk or some such."

"I'll look him up," Burmore said, as he finished his food and pushed away his plate.

"Tell him I said hello if you see him," David added. "He left most of his stuff too. Also, I'll see if I can't scare ya up some clothes and have them sent over to the cabin."

Darkness settled over the forest and light-bugs illuminated the air with their dim yellow glow. The humidity was heavy, but the once oppressive heat was gone. They'd all drank plenty of wine, and after a long chat around the table, David bade them farewell while standing on the wooden porch

They followed a path through the pines. Burmore led the way as they snaked through the forest.

"Why is it getting so cold?" Genya asked.

"The heat of the day disappears in the desert regions quickly after dark. By midnight ice will form and anyone caught outside without shelter will die of exposure," Burmore told them.

"How can a hot place grow so cold so fast?" Crystal asked, as she snuggled into Tommy.

"It has something to do with the pressure," Tommy added.

"Actually, there's not a lot of thermal mass to hold the heat. All that sand out there cools fast when the sun goes down. Once the heat is gone, the only thing left is cold."

Burmore pointed into the dark at a dim lantern light. "We'll go to the cabin first, then I'm off to the bath. Any of you are welcome to join me."

"A bath would be most welcomed," Crystal stated.

"Count me in," Genya said.

"All of you then?" Burmore looked back at all those following him. They in turn looked at each other and then each nodded. Burmore chuckled. "A unanimous decision I see. This is a rarity in life – trust me."

After a few minutes they made it to the cabin; wooden beams held up the front porch roof, and a plain wooden door allowed access. A lone lantern gave off a yellow-orange hue lighting the doorway.

The wooden path bifurcated, one way leading into the woods, while the other made a radial arc right to the portico. Burmore reached for the latch, pulled it up and opened the door.

A moment later a match was lit and a lantern revealed several chairs, a roughhewn table, six mattresses rolled up, and stacked canned goods on a shelf in the kitchen. In the corner, a fireplace was dark and cold with the remnants of the last fire still in it.

"This takes me back," Burmore said just as a small furry critter ran past their feet and out the open door.

Genya screamed and leapt into Tommy's arms. Crystal ran and climbed onto the table, knocking the chairs all around. Geris bolted from the doorway into the woods.

Ella shook her head. "It was just a dwoling cat, you idiots!"

Crystal climbed down from the table. "I knew that... I really did..."

"Me too, I wasn't afraid," Genya added, as she got down from Tommy's arms. "Where's Geris?"

A moment later Geris entered, and they all looked at him.

"What?" he asked.

"If it's anything like my old cabin, the towels can be found in the closet in the second bedroom," Burmore said. "I'll see about getting some fresh clothes for us in the morning."

He lit another lamp and handed it to Leland. "Go fetch the towels. Tommy, see if there's a bar of soap in the kitchen. Girls, I'm sorry to say, we have no shampoo, scented oils, or salts to make your bath truly pleasant." He walked over to a darkened area and dragged a couch over and in front of the fireplace. "Geris, grab some wood from the porch and bring it here. I'll get a fire going for when we return."

As they left toward the bath, the fire was roaring and the windows flooded with light. The air was now very chilly. Droplets of condensation were freezing on every surface.

The girls hurried after the men as they made their way along the board-road to a set of multistory buildings. Steam was coming out from the door as Burmore opened it.

They entered a wide room with lockers all around.

"Get undressed, store your clothes in a locker, and follow me," Burmore said.

They moved down a long hallway with doors on either side. The temperature was warm and humid. Burmore handed the girls the soap and opened a door.

"Here you go, ladies. I figured you'd want some privacy from us men. When you're done with the soap, bring it over to this room." He pointed at a door just down the hallway.

Genya looked annoyed. "We're not going to stay together?"

"A little time to freshen up will do us some

good," Geris stated. "Away, safe from the inane babble of girls," he added with a lone chuckle.

Genya stuck out her tongue at Geris. "Ass," she muttered.

Burmore looked at the young man. "You'll make a wonderful diplomat someday," he said, not bothering to hide his sarcasm. He turned to the girls. "Enjoy your privacy, ladies."

The men went down the hall. As they entered, the bath came into view. It was twenty feet wide, made of wood, and resembled a giant water barrel. Steam flew into the cold air as the water churned within.

Burmore dropped his towel onto the decking and climbed into the tub. Tommy, Leland, and Geris followed.

"Oh – the gods of old," Leland said, as he sank into the pleasant hot water.

They each sat around the edge, and after a few silent minutes Tommy spoke.

"When were you here last?" he asked Burmore.

"Quite a few years ago," Burmore stated. He submerged and came back up. "Feels like two or three lifetimes ago..." He noticed the blank expressions on the lad's faces. "You're all young men," he murmured. They looked at him with some curious bemusement.

"What I mean to say is, you're all a bit green... to adventure." He smiled. "When I was your age, I'd fought a war, ran a store, fled the authorities, loved quite a few women, drank copious amounts of liquor, and even tried my hand at politics. I say this not as an insult, but to explain that a man's past should remain... in the past."

He looked over at Leland. "Why do you think those Burkers want you so bad?"

"They're after Geris and Ella I think," Leland said.

"Ya, they've been trying to get me and my sister since Tiquan," Geris added.

Burmore chuckled. "I don't think you've thought this through, men. The Burkers want what will make their enemies capitulate. Why do they want you?" He pointed at Geris, and Leland. "What strategic value will you provide to those bastards?"

Tommy shrugged. "Shipping?" he asked.

"Yes, good work!" Burmore nodded.

"They have my father and mother," Geris said, "but they don't have Ella and me."

"Why would that be important?" Burmore looked thoughtful.

"So Phol and Ciciro can't send supplies to Maugray," Leland chimed in.

"Or, adequate supplies at least," Tommy added. "The Burkers will win if the Maugray soldiers can't resupply."

The door to the room opened and Genya was standing framed in the door, fully nude.

"Here's the soap, boys." She tossed the bar into the tub. "When you've scrapped the stink off of you, let us know and we'll join you." She turned, and the hourglass shape of her firm buttock wiggled as she exited. The door closed behind her.

Burmore's eyes were wide. "I... I had no idea," he stammered.

Tommy laughed. "I know what you mean."

Tommy took up the soap, and lathered all over. He washed thoroughly, then handed the soap to Leland.

Each man washed the sweat and grime from their bodies. After a while the door to the room opened again, and Ella stood there wrapped in a towel. Behind her were Genya and Crystal, and another woman.

Chapter 9

Report to High Command: Made Harrow's Gate passage and have transitioned to the desert. Desert troops have been deployed, and the town of Harrow's Gate will be pacified. No sighting of the rogue airship. Taking a contingent north toward unmapped Freelander settlements. End report.

***

Burmore stood up. "Katrina," he said. "I… this is… what I mean is—"

"Save your breath, Carl," she said. "You're lucky I don't drop a squib in there with you." Her eyes narrowed.

"A squib?" Tommy said.

"Come on, baby… you don't want to hurt these other people, do you?" Burmore had a panicked sound in his voice. "Think of the good times."

"What's a squib?" asked Geris.

Katrina stood on the decking next to the tub, put her hands on her hips, and leered down toward Burmore.

"It's a tiny creature that will swim up a man's penis and lay its eggs in his scrotum. When they hatch, they make a home inside the person and eat whatever they can find in there."

Geris stood up too and looked as if he'd leap from the barrel. Tommy and Leland also looked on the verge of panic.

Katrina stepped closer and crouched down.

"But I didn't have time to catch a squib just for you. When you and your…" she gave a serious look to each in the bath, "young friends here get done, I'll be waiting in your cabin. You've got a lot to make up for!"

She turned to leave, but glanced back over her shoulder. "Don't you think?" she added and left the room. The sound of her boots dissipated into the distance.

Burmore sat back into the hot water. "She gave me a start. I thought she had a squib and was going to drop it in." He chuckled softly, then noticed the others looking at him. "What? That's just foreplay. She's really a very sweet woman."

"What in the name of Height's Hell did you do to her?" Ella's voice was a combination of miffed and curious.

"Last time I was here, we had a tryst… of sorts. She's probably a bit annoyed that I left without telling her goodbye," Burmore said.

"She's more than annoyed it sounded," Crystal chimed in. "There's got to be more than that."

"We'll, we sort of were going to get married, but I had to high-tail it out of here. There was this nasty bit of business up north, and this bounty hunter came calling for me. I… I had to get out of town quick, and sort of left her at the altar."

"Now I see," Ella said. "I'd want to harm your privates too," she added.

"Not a very gentlemanly way to behave," Genya exclaimed.

"I think I see you in a different light,"

Crystal said.

All three girls turned on their heels and left the room.

Ella appeared back in the doorway. "We'll be back at the cabin. Perhaps Katrina will have more to tell us."

They left and the door slammed behind them.

"Damn. That made a mess of things," Tommy said. "Now what? Do we go after them?"

Burmore shook his head. "No, the best thing for us to do is let them get it out of their system. The later we show up at the cabin, the better. They'll be too tired to lash us much once we return. Diminish the beating, I always say."

After a few hours Burmore climbed out. "Get your wrinkly hides moving, lads. I guess we should go home and face the wrath."

"There're probably asleep by now," Leland suggested.

"If you think that my good man, I think you'll be unpleasantly surprised," Geris added.

Tommy climbed out and dried off. "I think that's wishful thinking too, and the savagery we're about to face is not going to be pretty."

They went back down the hall, into the locker room, and put on their clothes. Each, in turn, filed out into the biting cold, following the wooden road back to the cabin. As they approached, it was clear the girls were not asleep. Laughter was bubbling from the dwelling and lamplight caused an eerie yellow glow from all the windows.

Burmore stepped onto the porch. The laughing inside the cabin stopped, and he heard movement within. Putting his hand on the latch, the skyship captain exhaled, flipped up the handle, and opened the door.

"Here goes everything," he said.

The room was a little smoky. Ella, Genya, Crystal, and Katrina were nowhere to be seen. He and the others quickly moved to the fireplace. Burmore looked around and noticed the hallway to the bedrooms dark and quiet.

"They're waiting for us," he said.

"What do you mean?" Tommy asked.

Leland shook his head. "They want us to suffer, especially after Katrina told them all that Burmore did to her."

"You're a wise young man," Burmore said. "They're waiting all right, and I don't mind the wait. I'm just concerned about what will happen after they decide the waiting is over; that worries me quite a lot."

Geris sat down. "I'm sure none of it will concern me. You forget that I know Crystal, and Genya well, and I don't fancy either. If you keep them to yourself Tommy, I'll be all the happier."

"You're a strange fellow, Geris," Tommy said. "But who am I to argue?" Tommy began to wander down the hall. The boards creaked under his weight. He approached the first wooden door and reached for the latch.

"Next door, young blood," Katrina's voice range out.

Tommy let go the handle, turned and moved

down the hall to the next door. He laid his hand on it, and opened it. It was quiet, black, and cold. He exhaled softly. A voice, barely audible came from the bed.

"Get in here and close that door. We have one place for you tonight, and it's in the middle."

"You've been a bad boy, I think," Genya said.

Tommy swallowed hard, looked back into the main room, then back into the bedroom. He entered and shut the door behind him.

"That's a brave soul," Burmore said. He looked at Leland and Geris. "I guess I have to take some lumps if we're to stay here a couple of days. Wish me luck." He moved down the hall and opened the first door.

"You're a morg," Katrina's voice rose from the darkness. "You're a filthy, stinking, morg who's been very, very naughty."

Burmore looked back out the door to Leland. "Gimmely and galore, one foot in the pantry, and the other through the door," he said quoting from a children's nursery rhyme as he entered and closed the door.

Geris smiled. "Maybe you'd like to sleep in here with me tonight."

Leland smirked. "Ella's waiting."

"She'll tear you apart if she's angry. She almost took my head off with a vase in Tiquan," Geris said.

"I'll have to take my chances. I think Katrina has unbalanced our party, but they're giving us a chance tonight to make things right."

Leland left the fire and moved down the hallway. At the end was a door. He opened it. A white glow was coming in from the window. A biting cold hung in the air. He saw the bed. Under the covers lay Ella.

His blood was running hot, even as he stepped lightly toward the bed. She moved under the blankets.

"We're a long way from our parents and regular lives," Ella said. "Being timid does not win a lady's heart… or her body."

He boldly stepped to the bed and sat next to her. She moved slightly, then opened the comforter exposing a space for him. His heart raced and his mouth became dry.

He moved his hand under and along her bare shoulders. She shivered under his touch, but did not despair. His hand felt as if it were on fire, as his breathing became labored.

"Don't take all night, or you might miss your chance," she softly said. "We'll stay warmer if you lose those awful trousers and shirt."

In the air was the soft scent of pine and wood smoke. She threw the covers wide to expose her resplendent form. He pulled his shirt over his head, all the while Ella watched him intensely.

Her hands appeared on his abdomen, and she kissed him softly. He drew in the cool air through his nose, as she unlatched his belt, and unbuttoned his trousers. Soon, the garment lay with the others, cold and in shadow, upon the floor.

She rolled onto her side facing away from him. His arms engulfed her, and he pulled her in tightly to him. A subtle sigh escaped Ella's lips as she put her head back and he kissed her naked neck. The strong taste of salt invaded Leland's tongue, and his mouth glided over her shoulder, and along the back of her arm. Then, he planted soft kisses between her shoulder blades. She turned to face him.

The light of the moon filled the window. In the air was steam, driven from lungs that churned out the passionate mist. The sweat of their bodies glistened in the silvery moonlight. A desperate, unrestrained cry broke out into the night.

She put her head onto his chest. He felt as if his heart would burst. She lifted her head, looked up, and he was lost in her eyes.

"Let's do that again," she said.

"If this is punishment, I'll misbehave more often," Leland said under his breath.

"Then, misbehave," Ella told him.

Chapter 10

Report to High Command: Destination Kipper's Grove; the last stop going north. Estimated arrival: 1100 hours. The captain has determined it could be the most likely place the rogue airship would land if they made it over the mountain. End report.

***

Leland woke to a stifling heat. The window to the bedroom was filled with sunlight. The covers and comforter were on the floor in a tangled pile. Ella was asleep next to him, her nude body covered in glistening beads of sweat.

Pulling his arm from under her, he carefully got up, put on his trousers, and went out into the hall. The smell of brewing ayenda beans made him hunger for breakfast, and a cup of the black liquid he knew would do him well.

At the end of the hall he saw Geris sitting on the couch, Tommy was by the cold fireplace and Burmore at the stove.

"You look played-out but not broken!" Burmore laughed. "She went easy on you I see."

Leland smiled. "A gentleman keeps those details to himself." He took a seat at the table. "What are you cooking? It smells exquisite."

"Chilihorns, yoke plant, mine-shrooms and temper root," Burmore said. "Plenty for all."

"I smell ayenda," Ella said as she came down the hall wrapped in the bed sheet.

"Have a cup," Burmore said, as he handed her a mug and poured her a full cup of the bitter, oily liquid.

Ella took a sip. "Wow, that's amazing. I've never had it taste like this before."

"That's because it's pure and fresh, grown up on the hill by the snowline. David has a roasting house, and everyone here has a hand-grinder," Burmore said.

Crystal and Genya came from the hall, followed by Katrina. Katrina came to the table and sat down, her long work shirt barely covering the bottom of her buttocks. Crystal and Genya were in their underclothes. They both looked worn from lack of sleep. Genya approached Tommy and hugged him for quite a long time. Crystal went for a cup of ayenda, then went over to the couch and sat down next to Geris.

"I won't tell you what you smell like," Geris jibbed.

"Shut up, Geirs," Crystal said.

Burmore took the large skillet and sat it on a cozy on the table. "Grab a plate and dig in. I suspect we'll not get many chances to have such an exotic home cooked meal once we leave here."

"Leave?" Katrina asked.

"I'm taking these young folks down to Harrow's Gate and then down to the Pohl border. They have family there."

"Carl, you're not leaving me again, not like the last time. I'm coming too!" Katrina narrowed her gaze at him.

Burmore shook his head. "You don't know

what you're getting into… never mind. I forgot how stubborn you can be. You're welcome to come, but pack light."

Katrina smiled. "That's more like it. All I need is a change of clothes and my scatter-gun"

Burmore smiled. "That's my girl," he said. "Now, let's eat."

They all sat down at the table and ate. The food was hearty, and the ayenda hot and satisfying. Several conversations broke out, but they all came back to, how to stay ahead of the Burkers.

When the dishes were done, and they'd all sat about feeling the rising heat of the day, Burmore stood.

"I'm going to take a walk back to the bathhouse to clean up. You're all welcome to join me," he said.

The frigid-pools were little more than siphoned brook water. Burmore climbed into one of the tubs and began lathering with soap.

"If you don't mind me asking, Carl, what are we going to do next?" Ella asked as she dropped her towel, and stepped into the large round tub.

"I'm sure those Burkers have given up by now. All they saw was us going into that cloud, and I have a good feeling that they've headed off to greener pastures. I figured we'd take a couple of days here; get some rest, stow some supplies and then float on down to Harrow's Gate. Two days at the Gate, then make for the Phol border and the Lake Country."

He walked over to the soap and commenced

to washing.

Katrina let go her towel and stepped into the tub, as did Crystal and Genya.

Leland, Tommy, and Geris came into the room.

"After we scrub-up, we need to go find some supplies," Burmore said. "We should let these beautiful ladies relax for a bit."

Garis laughed. "At least it'll keep them out of our hair."

The women began chatting, as the men stepped out of the tub. Once dried off, Burmore climbed the stairs to the door.

"Go back to the cabin. David was supposed to find some extra clothes for us. Gather them up and meet me at the landing zone," he told Leland, Tommy, and Geris.

The men left the bath. The women continued to wash and discuss aspects of the journey, and the perils that might lay ahead.

***

The heat was becoming nearly unbearable when Leland reached the cabin. Rays of light came down from the trees illuminating the ground and the red-brown dust which moved about suspended in the air. He opened the door and bowed slightly to Tommy and Geris.

"By all means, please come in."

In the back room Leland found some fresh clothes on the bed. He put them on and was surprised to see that they fit pretty well. For a moment he gazed down at the finely made dress that was laid out. In his mind he saw Ella within.

Going back out into the living room, he found Geris and Tommy, also in new clothes. "There are a couple of dresses in there," Tommy said.

"And shoes," Geris added.

"Who do you think put them there?" Tommy asked.

"Grab it all up and let's drop off the clothes to the girls and get over to the ship and give Burmore a hand."

They left the cabin and walked back to the washhouse. Leland let the women know they'd brought the clothes, they then set out back along the wooden road toward the landing zone.

As they passed the cabin, the sound of boots atop the wooden road rushed toward them. Leland looked up to see Burmore in a mad dash coming straight at them.

"Run!" Burmore shouted, as he sprinted past them toward the cabin.

Without a question they all three turned on their heels and pursued the man. Leland saw Burmore approaching the cabin, but he did not stop there.

"What's this about?" Leland called out.

"The Burkers… they've landed at the harbor, in force," Burmore shouted back. He ran to the bathhouse and nearly collided with Katrina coming out.

"Take the lads with you to the trading post," he frantically said.

The popping sound of gunfire echoed from the landing zone area.

Burmore looked back, then at Katrina. "Hurry, this place will be crawling with Burkers soldiers soon."

"What about your ship?" she asked.

"They're hovering right over it. We can't get out that way."

"What about Hobart Tapping Hole?" she asked.

"There's no way we can make it there on foot." Burmore grabbed her hand and began walking quickly.

"Farley bought a puffer a few years before he left. It's still in his shed," Katrina said.

Burmore stopped. "A puffer, in his shed?" He turned around and started leading them back. "Does it work?"

"He rode it to Harrow's gate and back in four days. But it's been idle for about five years now," Katrina said while holding the hem of her dress up so she moved faster.

"What's a puffer?" Tommy asked.

"I'll show you," Burmore said, "and I think you'll appreciate it."

Burmore stopped at a large wooden out-building not far from Farley's cabin. The sound of gunfire was not far off. He opened a sliding door and looked into the building.

Miscellaneous junk was strewn about and wooden boxes were stacked high. Just peeking out from under a pile he saw the arch of a metal wheel. He grabbed a handful of loose items and threw them outside. He then pulled out a box and tossed it outside too.

"Come on, grab and toss!" Burmore said.

After a few moments they'd uncovered the front end of the vehicle.

"Pull," Burmore ordered.

Each found a place to grab. Burmore's face turned red as he strained. Leland grunted, Tommy growled, and the others heaved, as the craft came rolling out.

It was fifteen feet long and ten feet wide. There was a wooden shell where the driver and passengers sat, but the rest was made of metal, including the spoke wheels.

Down the middle was a container like the one on Burmore's ship, but bigger. Attached to the wheels were metal arms designed to drive them. In some ways, it looked like the mechanics of a steam-wheel.

Burmore climbed up into the vehicle and opened a leather chest.

"Thank the gods; he purchased a full box of fuel rods." He sat in the seat and took a hold of the lever controller rods. "Push us over to the creek."

Leland, Tommy, and Geris pushed the metal contraption down an incline to the water. Behind them there was more shooting and shouting.

Once the craft was at the bottom, Burmore unrolled a hose, took hold of a lever, and started to pump. After a few minutes, he stopped and secured the hose then went to the box. He took out a metal rod and slipped it into a tube that led into the water reservoir.

"Get in," Burmore said as he locked in the

rod. "Find a place to hang on. I've only driven a puffer once, so let's hope—"

"Stop, you there!" shouted someone back by the cabin.

"It's soldiers," Leland said just as projectiles glanced off the metal skeleton and whizzed off into the woods. "Go!"

Burmore pulled out a knob and steam erupted on each side. The arms moved, metal screeched, and the wheels began to turn. Dust and pine needles flew back and into the air. Men were rushing down and shouting at them.

Burmore pulled a handle on a chain and a whistle blared as the craft took off, leaving a trail of dust and debris behind it.

"Hold on," Burmore shouted as the craft hurtled through the woods. He pulled the control levers, and used his feet on the drive peddles as the vehicle smashed through brush and over ruts. The puffer passed through a clearing, and down a wide path. The wind was blasting them, and Burmore's eyes were tearing as the craft raced on.

He maneuvered around corners and down berms and wadis. The vibration was savage, and Burmore fought to control the vehicle, frantically pulling small levers, and adjusting pull-knobs and valves.

The puffer emerged from the forest and sped out into the desert. Instantly the heat of the sun blasted them.

They flew along dry riverbeds and over a dusty plateau. Burmore loosened the strings on his shirt which billowed out. He felt the trickle of sweat

down his back, and the sun burning his face. He
fought his own terror as he controlled the metal
monster.

There'd been no time to look for the puffer's
bonnet to cover the cabin. Burmore knew they'd not
last long under that cruel sun. He had to think of
something quickly, all the while he pulled levers
and smashed his feet against the pedals.

At one point he missed a dangerous incline,
then narrowly avoided a drop off. He had to think…
where to go to protect them from the sun? A tapping
hole would be their only hope, and the nearest one
was still quite a ways away. They'd have to make it;
if they didn't, they'd not be alive.

Chapter 11

Report to High Command: Burmore spotted at Kippler's Grove. Civilian agitators assaulted landing force. Report of a group fitting the description of the children escaped toward the desert in a puffer-car. Mounting a pursuit. Airship will attain altitude and we will search for their trail. End report.

***

Burmore glanced down at the distance-counter; thirty miles it read. They'd been exposed to the sun for thirty minutes now. The tapping hole was nearby, if he could just remember the landmarks.

Crystal groaned loudly then fell unconscious. Tommy and Genya tried to shield her from the sun's merciless rays. Katrina stripped off her dress and they held it over Crystal – though it whipped about in the mad wind.

The puffer-car smashed over ruts and holes as Burmore continued fighting to keep control of the fast craft; his forearms strained, the cords in his arm showing like steel strands as he adjusted the directional levers. The craft careened down a hill and into a wadi.

Try and remember, old chap, Burmore thought, *where is that tapping hole*. He came around the corner of an outcropping of white chalk cliffs and directly onto a well-worn path. Lashing at the controls, he fumbled for the break and pressure release to bring the puffer to a halt.

He simultaneously jerked the brake-lever, and released the drive-steam from the pistons. The wheels locked, the steam vented, and the puffer began sliding sideways. All except Burmore screamed in terror.

"Hold on!" Burmore shouted.

The craft spun around, and the puffer came to a tenuous halt right at the edge of a tapping hole.

The sky captain turned to the others. "Not bad for only driving one of these contraptions once before," he said, then realized the others were as pale as a desert ghost. "You guys okay?"

Katrina slowly shook her head. "I can't believe we're not dead."

Burmore looked over at the unconscious girl. "Come on, we have to get Crystal into the shade. I know the way down into this hole."

Leland climbed down; his legs were a bit wobbly.

"Hand Crystal here," he said.

He took her by the arms and eased her down to the dirty sand. Genya, Ella, Tommy, Geris, and Katrina climbed down, followed by Burmore.

Tommy and Leland carried Crystal, as they all followed Burmore along the rocky rim to a path carved into the side of the wide and deep hole. As they descended, the air became cooler.

Once at the bottom, they found a flat rim that ran around the deep blue pool of water that spanned more than a hundred feet.

The light from above reflected off the water and made abstract, almost luminescent images that shimmered along the walls. The grotto was more pleasant than they'd hoped.

Crystal was burned. Her face was puffy and in a few places blisters puckered up. As they assessed each other, they all displayed similar injuries from the trip.

"Damn it, Carl," Katrina said while looking at her reflection in the tapping pool. "You've made us all into burnt offerings!"

"Sorry, love, there was no choice in the matter," Burmore said. "If you preferred to stay with the Burkers, you should have spoken up."

She looked at him with a queer smile on her face. "You just called me love." Her mood changed. "I've so longed to hear you say those words to me again."

"Now what?" Geris asked. "We're stuck in this hole for the Burkers to find."

"I think they'll have a hell of a time finding us. Even I'm not sure how I got here," Burmore told them.

"We've got no food," Ella said.

"But we do have plenty of water." Tommy pointed at the entrancing pool.

"We're not without food," Burmore told them. "Ella and Leland, gather up a few of those old pottery jars." He pointed at some brown clay urns piled by a cavern opening. "Follow me. I'll show you where to find some excellent food for all of us." He began walking toward a large darkened hole in the rock face. "Give your eyes a few minutes to adjust," he added.

They followed Burmore into the blackness.

A few minutes later, a dim green glow began to illuminate the tunnel. It was as if the full moon were shining inside. Details came into view; the tunnel was tall, wide, and with squared and distinct walls.

"Looks like some sort of mine," Leland said.

"Many of these tapping holes have caves like this," Burmore told him.

"What is this glowing stuff?" Leland asked.

"These caves and caverns exhibit a green kind of luminescence. I'm not sure what causes it. One thing for certain, it gives off plenty of light. And it's not just in the tunnels. When the sun goes down tonight, be prepared for a sight that you'll keep close to your heart for a lifetime."

"What are we after in here?" Leland furthered.

"Shuma root, mushrooms, and khail slime."

"Slime?" Ella asked disgusted.

"It will temper our sunburns," Burmore said. "The Velenar used it on me years ago."

Burmore began walking deeper into the tunnel. They turned left at an intersection, walked for a while, then turned left again. Mushrooms grew along the base of the walls, and strange white roots protruded here and there. In some of the corners a slimy ooze dripped into puddles on the floor.

Burmore pointed to a group of mushrooms with glowing stripes along the cap. "Don't pick these." He then pointed at some that had iridescent purple spots on the cap. "These we can eat."

He pulled out a pocket knife and cut some long, white, beet-like roots protruding into the passageway. "These are good for eating too. Gather up an arm full. Fill the jars with the puddled slime, and we'll make our way back." He pulled up the bottom of his shirt and held the end with his teeth. He began to pluck up mushrooms and cut roots, and put them in the makeshift satchel.

"Who made these pots?" Ella asked.

"The desert people, long ago," Burmore mumbled with the cloth in his mouth "They're actually the size of a cup to them. All the tapping holes have these urns stacked near the tunnels. I think they used them for drinking the water."

"The desert ghosts come here?" Leland asked.

"This is their land. They were here long before we came," Burmore said. "They come and go as they please. Some may be observing us even as we speak." He looked about, then looked at Leland and Ella and smiled. "Come on; let's get back to the others."

They made their way back toward the tapping hole. Emerging into the dimming light was a bit unnerving. The sun had passed beyond the opening, and now a shadow shrouded the hole in darkness. Ella shivered and set down the two pots

"That tunnel gives me the creeps," she said.

"Funny, it didn't really bother me," Leland added.

Ella gave him a disapproving look.

The others had arranged the rocks so they had a small camp site laid out. Crystal had regained consciousness and was sitting up. She looked over and tried to smile, but stopped due to pain.

"Here, try this on those burns," Burmore

said and brought over a pot of slime.

"I don't want that on my face," Crystal protested. "It's disgusting!"

"Even if it'll prevent the formation of terrible scars?" Burmore narrowed his eyes at her.

Crystal looked up at him, then at the clay pot filled with the greenish ooze.

"Okay," she conceded. "I'll try it."

The evening was coming on. Burmore ascended to the top of the hole and hid the puffer near an outcropping of boulders. A powerful wind picked up as the temperature plummeted.

A few minutes later he came back down. He shivered as he found a place to sit.

"If those Burkers were relying on following our tracks, they have another thing coming." Burmore sat back, then struck up a flare he'd brought from the puffer.

Next to him was a pile of dried roots and tunnel vines, and he made a fire with them. The orange of the fire illuminated the water and the walls, and cast twisted and amorphous shadows on the rocks.

They roasted the white roots and toasted the mushrooms. The smell was intoxicating. They feasted on the vegetables and fungus until late in the night.

As the fire burnt down, they noticed at the rim of the tapping hole, icicles were forming. The wind made an eerie howl. Every once in a while bits of sand would shower down into the pool making a strange hissing sound.

Each of them put the slime on their burns. In

an instant, the pain vanished, and their skin felt as cool as the air. Burmore poked the fire with a stick, then sat back and watched the water.

Just about the time the last of the flames died, the cavern lit up. The iridescent green color pulsed and simmered from under the water, and the aggregate stone peppered with reflective metals sparkled in the night.

In the air, dark blue lights appeared and floated about, and in the water, dark purple lights moved and swam.

"What is this?" Genya asked.

"Each hole is a little different," Burmore began. "The Valenar People use the colors and patterns to tell where they are, or rather what the name of each tapping hole is."

Tommy looked surprised. "Name?"

"Yes." Burmore maneuvered a root out of the coals and onto a flat rock. He tore it open with his pocket knife, exposing the dark orange meat, and ate some of it. "This hole is called Chet Um Tolich," he said while pointing at glowing markings along the walls.

"How is it you know these things?" Ella asked.

"As I told you, I spent some time with them. Make sure you've put the slime on all your burns. By morning you'll be surprised. Now, try and get some sleep. Tomorrow, we'll have to haul up water in these jugs so we can refill and prime the puffer. Harrow's Gate is three days from here, and it's all desert in between."

Burmore lay back and closed his eyes.

Katrina came over and snuggled in next to him, putting her arms around his chest. She looked up at his handsome face, smiled, and closed her eyes too.

Chapter 12

Report to High Command: Airship recalled back to Kipper's Grove to help evacuate wounded infantry. Inhabitants of the mining camp provided fierce resistance. Once the evacuation was complete, ship returned to compass heading of target, but sandstorm caused the search to be called off. It is believed the puffer-car is in rout to Harrow's Gate. Will travel to Harrow's Gate and wait for targets. End Report.

***

It was still dark when Burmore woke the group. "We need to get an early start," he told them. "Carry up jars of water to the puffer and we'll refill the reservoir. Once we get going, the land will slope toward the far north and east. That means the White Desert will be visible to us. I want to hit the trail before the sun reaches it." He took a jar, filled it at the pool, put it on his shoulder, and marched up the small pathway to the top.

It took many trips each to carry enough water to refill the chamber on the car. Each of them climbed into the rig and made ready to travel. Burmore handed two extra jars to Leland and Tommy.

"We'll need this for hydration," Burmore said. He inserted a fuel rod and locked it in place.

"Hold on," he said as he got into the control seat.

He looked over his shoulder as he let off the break, activated the heating chamber, and engaged the forward controller. He held firmly onto the

137

steering levers and the craft began to move along the dusty wadi.

As the sun rose, the cold of the morning was washed away, and the stifling heat began to build. For the most part they stayed down in the valleys. On the rare occasion when Burmore had to bring them up onto a ridge, they saw a sharp white light in the distance.

Coming around a large hillside, Burmore pulled back on the left turn lever and the craft again glided around a pile of debris. Ahead the wadi grew wide.

The puffer emerged into the light of the rising sun. They were now on a wide mesa. In the east the sun breached the far flung mountains and in the distance the white desert erupted with blinding light. Each of them covered their eyes, except Burmore, who took out a pair of dark-lensed glasses and put them on.

He opened the steam throttle and the craft picked up speed.

"I know where I'm going now," Burmore said. "I hope we can make it to the Valence Tapping Hole by noon. There we can wait out the rest of the day. Tonight we'll try and make the next tapping hole, and then on to Harrow's Gate; the moon will be out, and driving should be easy."

They drove on through the morning until the sun grew savage. Burnmore glided down a hill and into another wide wadi. He slowed the vehicle, came around a pile of tan boulders, and stopped the puffer.

After securing the break, he released the

steam from the cylinders and climbed out. Removing his glasses; his eye sockets appeared as two round clean spots on a filthy dust covered face.

"The tapping hole is this way."

The path into the hole was similar to the last one; a path along the wall that led all the way down to the pool.

Ella gathered drinking water into a couple of jugs, then stripped down and climbed into the water. Genya and Crystal followed. It took little instigation to tempt Katrina, Burmore, Tommy, and Leland into the cool waters. They all swam for some time, playing in the shallows and diving off rocks.

Burmore climbed from the water and dried. "Ella, Leland, see if you can find some mushrooms and roots in the tunnel." He pointed at a looming dark hole fifteen feet high, and at least half that wide.

"By ourselves?" Ella asked.

Leland climbed out and dried, then put on his clothes. "Come on. I'll be with you. What could happen?"

Ella swam to the shallows and stood up. As she got to the shore she looked at the cavern. "I'm worried; that's my prerogative!" she said. "What if there's some angry obar in there, or a hungry something else?"

Leland chuckled and took her by the hand. "We'll be fine. Come on."

As they proceeded along the passageway, the voices of their friends grew fainter. In the green glow they soon came across some of the beet-roots protruding from the cavern walls.

"I feel like something is watching us," Ella said pointing down a connecting tunnel.

"Nonsense, it's all in your mind," Leland stated.

"I'll remember that you said that," she said, and turned down a connecting passage. She stopped, and slowly backed up.

Leland saw a look of terror on her face as she backed all the way to the tunnel wall. From the opening came a figure. It looked human, but was three times as tall as Leland and wore a flowing robe that glowed green. The creature's bare hands and sandaled feet also radiated bright green. It came into the passage and looked down on Leland and Ella.

"Cum'a titsu comoteh," it said.

"We don't understand your language," Leland said.

Ella ran to Leland. "Look at the size of it."

"I am not an *it*. I am a *he*. It is clear that you do not know the greeting of The People. Say it with me, Cum'a titsu, comoteh," he repeated.

Leland said it back.

The tall man laughed. "Your accent is good. Remember those words and you will be respected among The People. How came you, a human female and male, to this place?"

"We were searching for roots and mushrooms to eat," Leland said.

"I am Her'ao sage of clan Uden. Do not be afraid, I am peaceful. Did you come from the sacred pool?"

"We did. There are more of us there…"

Leland winced as Ella pinched his arm. "Hey, stop that," he said to her.

"It's okay. She's afraid that I will do you and your friends harm. I will not. Now, gather up your supplies; I'll help you. When done, I'll introduce myself to your friends." He began searching around the walls of the tunnel, and picking roots and mushrooms and putting them into a cloth sack he carried around his shoulder.

They gathered a bountiful amount of food, then began walking back toward the tapping hole.

"The dark will come soon, and with it the cold. I'll show you how to use the fire-stones to heat your food and keep you warm in the cold night," Her'ao told them over his shoulder.

They emerged from the cavern opening. Crystal screamed, and Genya grabbed up a rock. Geris gasped and ran up the trail toward the desert above.

Burmore turned to look. His expression turned to a grin.

"Her'ao!" he said.

"Ah, now I see why there are humans in this sacred pool," Her'ao said with a chuckle.

Burmore bowed. "Cum'a titsu comoteh," he said.

"You remembered the words well," Her'ao said as he came to the fire and sat down cross-legged. "Sauru cum'a etu.".

"Sauru," Burmore said while raising his left hand, palm out. He approached the giant and sat opposite. "How is it that you are here?"

Her'ao looked around at the still shocked

group. "A question I have for you too. Perhaps it is the same answer, and perhaps it isn't?"

"We're running for our lives," Burmore said. "A war has started west of the divide. I fear there will be much killing before it's done."

Her'ao lay back against a set of rocks. "It seems the way of you humans; to kill and ruin. I am disappointed." He put his legs straight out and put his feet by the fire. "But we share a common reason for being here. Mao'te asked me to seek guidance at the sacred pool. He fears that your war may force our people to stay in the desert until you are done. I must ask tonight when the Mech aught en'naugh rises from the pool."

"What is a Mech aught en'naugh?" Geris asked coming back down to the ramp.

"I believe your people use the word oracle," Her'ao said.

"Can we watch?" Genya asked.

"If you like. When the moon is above this tapping hole, I'll call upon the Mech aught en'naugh. It will know what is happening." He looked over at Leland and Ella. "Ah, I almost forgot to show you the fire-stones. This fire is well and good, but in many of the ancient holes there are no combustibles.

"A fire cannot be made at those locations. In the old times, my people used the chara chan to warm food and keep warm. We made them after the Leaving. Look and when you are at another sacred pool, do as I do."

Her'ao stood and went to a pile of stones. He looked through them, then pulled out one white, and one black. There were opposite right angle cuts in each. He approached the fire and sat down again. Taking the two stones he fitted them together and set them on the ground. He piled some rocks around it and waited. The pile began to glow red. Heat waves distorted the image of the pool behind it. Taking some of the mushrooms, he set them against the rock pile and looked at the assembled group.

"It is done," he said. "Bring your roots to bake, and place them along the sides with the mushrooms."

"How long will it burn?" Tommy asked.

"It doesn't actually burn. But, it will heat long enough to keep warm by and to cook food. By the morning, the stones will part and cool. Leave them for another traveler to use, and go about your way."

Burmore lay back and beckoned Katrina to come sit by his side.

"Her'ao is a holy man. He knows the way to summon the water spirit. When I was with his people he showed me the Mech aught en'naugh." He looked at the others. "Don't be afraid of it when you see it. It won't harm you."

The strong smell of roasting mushrooms and baking tubers filled the air. Geris, Tommy, Genya, and Crystal came closer to the hot stones.

"Where are your people now?" Crystal asked.

"They are at the place you call Harrow's Gate. My people call it…" he looked thoughtful for a moment, "the Engineers Arch."

"Engineers?" Tommy almost smiled at the

mention of the word.

"My people worked many a lifetime for the Engineers who came and made the White Desert. We worked for them and mined many worlds searching for the resources to build the Edeon Spiral Enclaves. After the Engineers abandoned us on this world, my father was contacted by the Mech aught en'naugh. I carry on this tradition."

"We don't know any of those names, or even what you're talking about," Genya said.

Her'ao chuckled. "Did you not tell them anything of what you learned," he said to Burmore.

"They wouldn't believe it if I told them. I'm not sure I believe it," Burmore added.

"Then eat, and relax. The moon will be overhead soon, and you will all see an amazing sight."

Her'ao sat up as several mushrooms made a popping sound and fell from the heating stones. They looked ridiculously small in his large hand as he picked each up by the stem and ate them.

With some trepidation, they all consumed the bounty. Slowly, the tension vanished and as the green moon became visible in the corner of the opening, each person asked Her'ao questions about his people, their ways, and their language.

"I am of the Eyo Velenar people; those who worked to consume worlds for the Engineers. The Engineers left suddenly, and when they did, they left us behind."

"Where did they go?" Geris asked.

"None of us know. One day the harvesters and processors were overhead, and the next they were gone."

"What did you do for them?" asked Leland.

"It was our job to search out the precious resources they needed. The work made deserts of many a wandering world. Upon much reflection – it was a task that we regret and are now ashamed. All worlds should be free of molestation – to let the life within it be.

"After they left my father discovered the Mech aught en'naugh. It spoke of a bridge between this world and the Green Moon; a way for us to find ships the Engineers had forsaken, so we can return home."

"You live on the moon?" Crystal asked.

"Not exactly. There are ships there that can take us back home, provided we can get to it." Her'ao looked at Ella and smiled. "Your people do not understand yet. We have learned over the years that humans on this coast do not have an understanding of such things. And if you continue to fight, you will again fall into a primitive state."

"Again?" Geris asked.

"Yes – again," Her'ao said.

"What nonsense! The Green Moon, and moon-ships?" Geris blurted.

Leland ate some root, then sat by the pool. "What exactly is the Mech aught en'naugh?" he asked.

"What? Who? Where? When? It is all these things. It dwells far beyond this world. You will be able to ask soon any question you want answers to." Her'ao looked up and noted the large green orb moving toward the center of the hole.

"I will summon it soon. I have brought some herbs to help ease the experience. Consume them, then sit quietly around the pool." Her'ao handed them some green fuzzy stems.

Burmore took a sprig and popped it into his mouth. Chewing, he motioned for the other to do the same. They all did.

Leland sat and watched. Light from the green moon flooded into the hole. After a few minutes it grew more intense. Soon, the color made the night sky blaze with green light.

A sound rose from Her'ao; first melodious, then rhythmic. Bugs emerged from the water, buzzing this way and that. Slowly, they began to glow. Leland's ears buzzed too, with a pleasing sound.

The light-bugs flew to Her'ao and landed on him. He was awash with them. In the middle of the pool something formed, hovering just above it. A bipedal creature with four arms and a trunk for a nose appeared. The creature lifted its trunk. A yellowish beak moved.

Her'ao stopped his harmony and spoke in his tribal language. This went on for some time, as stars passed overhead and the light-bugs buzzed in everyone's ears.

When the reflection of the green moon was nearly to the other side of the pool, the glow-bugs left Her'ao and flew all around again.

Her'ao turned to the rest of the group. "The Mech aught en'naugh has asked for you Leland Niva."

Leland felt strange, almost drunk as the

shifting colors swam all around him. He got to his feet and came forward. The glow-bugs came and landed all over his exposed skin.

He couldn't see clearly for all the bright yellow light. The buzzing faded, and so did the light. For a moment he was disoriented.

The tapping hole was gone, his friends were gone, Her'ao was gone. He saw the Mech aught en'naugh standing on a broad plateau covered in blazing red grass. The sky was a crystal blue with white clouds.

"I have tapped into your primitive processor. This is to ease your fear. It is made up of colors that you feel are calming. Is it so?" the Mech aught en'naugh asked.

Leland felt a jolt of fear run up his spine, but just as quickly he calmed; the colors were indeed pleasing. "It has that effect," he said. "This is not real?"

"Real?" The beak of the creature gnashed up and down. "In the state you are in, you can't comprehend the truth of 'real'. Suffice to say, you see only a fraction of all that is or ever was."

"You speak in riddles. Are you trying to confuse me?"

Again the beak gnashed. "No, just being honest. It is not in my nature to cause you such confusion"

Leland walked around for a moment and felt the grass. "What exactly are you, and where do you come from?"

"Once, there was a race of beings that sought to catalogue the whole of the universe. They made me. I extend into the past which you perceive, and reside in the present, and dwell far into the coming constructions of what you would call the future." The creature turned and walked a short distance, then motioned with one of its hands for Leland to follow.

They walked for some distance until they were at the edge of the mesa. Below, a splendid city was constructed. Mile high twisting spires loomed over many smaller structures. What looked like oddly shaped steam wheels buzzed about over the ground, and in the air were flying machines without balloons.

"What is this place?" Leland asked.

"A place that will not cause you to panic," the Mech aught en'augh said. "I have a request of you. I am in need of your help. In return, I will give you help to rescue your friends from those that have taken them. If you will permit me, I will connect myself to you in a permanent way. This will allow you to call upon me, and I you, at any time. No others will know, see, or hear me."

"What do you want me to do for you?"

The Mech aught en'naugh's eyes narrowed slightly.

"Your people enshrined a device that is far older than your race. They did not know its value or power. You must go and put it back on-line, so I might help the Valenar to seek their home."

"Why haven't you sent a Valenar to do this thing for you?"

"They are not the builders of the shrine. They would not be permitted to enter. You, Leland

Niva can."

Leland came around the creature and looked up at its face. "What of Ella's father and mother, and Tommy's dad, Carter?"

"They will be freed," the Mech aught en'naugh said.

"How will they be freed?"

"You will free them." The creature's beak gnashed up and down. "In the desert there is a machine that can deliver you to the prison in Tiquan where they are kept. It was damaged long ago, but can still fly. I will help you fly it to rescue your friends."

Leland walked around for a moment, then turned to the creature. "Okay, I'll help you. Now, what do I do?"

"With your permission, I shall connect to your mind."

"Do what you need to do," Leland told the Mech aught en'naugh.

"You will feel momentarily disoriented, then normal." The creature's arms moved about, and blobs of color seemed to fill the air like ink in a bucket of water.

Leland's vision cleared and he realized he was in the tapping hole. He was standing on the edge of the pool as the glow-bugs flew away, and then mixed with the water until they'd all vanished.

Leland looked at his friends. "I was in a foreign place. There was red grass, and a sapphire-blue sky. It was as real as this is now. How long was I—?"

"Covered in bugs? Only for a minute,"

Burmore said.

"It seemed I was there for a long time," Leland told them.

"What did the Mech aught en'naugh say to you?" Her'ao asked.

"It wants me to do a task for it. Do you understand any of that?"

Her'ao thought for a moment. "The Mech aught en'naugh speaks in riddles often to my people. I guess the truth will be revealed in time, for its predictions always come true."

Leland shrugged his shoulders. "Why would it speak in riddles?"

Her'ao laughed. "I cannot say, but it has burdened my people with trying to think of what it intends for us to do. I can only surmise that it must love mystery."

Ella chuckled. "Did any of you stop to think that it might be a female?"

Leland looked surprised. "It never crossed my mind, but now that you mention it I can see that."

"We do love our secrets and mysteries," Ella said.

"If you wish, "Her'ao began, I can lead you to Harrow's Gate by the tunnels? You'll stay out of the sun, and dry desert air."

Burmore looked at his young companions, then at Katrina. He knew the desert posed many dangers that could be bypassed if they had a guide in the tunnels.

"That would be very kind of you," Burmore said to Her'ao. "We'll go with you through the tunnels."

Chapter 13

Report to High Command: Five command airships have taken up positions around Harrow's Gate. No avenue of approach is hidden. Ground deployment successful and inhabitants pacified. Large gathering of Valenar people at Gate. Advise. End Report

***

Her'ao led the way through the tunnel. They were all exhausted. At a wide opening he stopped.

"We will rest here for a time." He sat down. "The access to the surface is still a ways off."

"Access?" Genya asked.

"Long ago, before your people came to the Augerland, the Engineers had us build access ways to and from the surface. We built much for the Engineers here on this world. We made the tapping holes, and the connecting tunnels. We also made passages that connect to key places on the surface. You will see one of the old tunnels soon." He leaned back, folded his arms over his chest, and closed his eyes.

"Who are the Engineers?" Tommy asked.

Her'ao didn't open his eyes. "Not an easy question to answer. In all my years of service, I never saw one. They encased themselves in machines."

"Why?" Geirs asked.

"To find the elements that they used to make their ships, goods, homes, and other amazing things," Her'ao said.

"Where do you think they are now?" Crystal

asked.

"It was unusual that they'd leave us in a place like this, but they did. We have speculated for many years on the matter, but don't have sufficient evidence to support any conclusion. There is only hypothesis."

"What is your hypothesis?" Leland asked.

"Some disaster happened; a collapse of their civilization maybe, or perhaps war. One fact is, they took all of their working processing machines and flew away."

"What did they leave behind?" Geris asked.

"Some damaged pieces that wouldn't make the journey back into orbit."

"What do you mean orbit? Like circling around an object?" Leland asked.

Her'ao nodded his head. "That place that your scientists watch with telescopes. That is where they went. Up there."

"Impossible!" Geris stated.

"You're having us on," Tommy said.

"He's not," Burmore added. "There is a mystery here, vastly more complex than I ever wanted to tackle."

"We still have some distance to travel, so you'd better get some rest," Her'ao said, then he clasped his fingers over his chest and became quiet.

The tunnel fell into silence. Leland closed his eyes and drifted off into a deep and dreamless sleep. He came back awake when Ella nudged him.

"Time to go," Ella said.

Leland looked at her. "Did you get some sleep?" He rubbed his eyes.

"Some."

Her'ao stood up and waited for the others, then turned and walked down the tunnel. They followed for a long time until Tommy's stomach growled loudly, and Crystal began to complain about hunger pains. Ahead, the tunnel split off.

"This way," Her'ao said, and took the path that seemed to angle upward.

They walked for a hundred yards and stepped out onto a metal platform that clanked underfoot. Her'ao pointed at a set of metallic stairs leading up.

"That way leads to the temple at Harrow's Gate," he said. "I'm heading to my father's encampment at the Khi'ahu tapping hole in this direction. I'm sorry that our paths diverge here. May you know the Maker's purpose, and go in peace to seek your way." He bowed slightly and looked at them with a smile, before turning and vanishing into the low light of the passageway.

They listened as Her'ao's footsteps became less and less, until they couldn't be heard at all.

Burmore took the lead. Slowly they made their way up the metal stairway. Along the way Leland saw strange patterns in the walls, odd geometric patterns that he'd never seen before.

They came to a wide landing, much bigger than the others. At one end was a tall and wide metal door with a spiral locking mechanism, much like that on a ship. Burmore approached it and cranked it counter clockwise. A clicking sound was heard and he pulled the door inward.

They saw stone stairs. Fixed to the wall at

intervals were white electric lights all the way up. After what seemed like an hour, they emerged into a circular room covered by a dome ceiling fitted with glass. Burmore approached a wooden door.

The hinges were rusty and the brass handle tarnished. He gripped the handle and pulled. The door came inward exposing a small room with another door. A metal rod was across the jam locking the portal. Burmore slid the iron bar, unlocked the door, and pulled.

Beyond that door was a tall hallway with a vaulted roof. The floor was lined with tile, and the walls appeared to be stucco. From down the hall he heard footsteps and talking; the sound was coming toward them. He closed the door and listened. The sounds passed.

Looking out, he saw two men in blue uniforms turn a corner and vanish.

"Come on," Burmore said and entered the hallway.

At the far end he saw a set of double doors made of wood and strapped with bronze and copper. Geris was the last one out and he closed the door softly.

Around the corner came a Burker with a messenger bag. He came to a skidding halt.

"Who are you?" he demanded, his Burker accent thick.

Burmore glanced back at the others then addressed the man with an equally strong accent.

"These people, I have arrested them. My name is Heist Von Gutenbach, major with the suspol intelligence police." He slowly reached into his pants pocket and produced a billfold.

Handing the wallet out to the Burker, he smiled and nodded at the wallet.

The man reached for it, only to find Burmore's fist aside his jaw. The soldier dropped like a wet sack of sand. Crystal gasped, and Genya squeaked with fear. Burmore straddled the man, searched him quickly, then took his satchel and pistol.

He went down the hall and threw open the next door. He sprinted down a side passage that ended at a wide garden. Ahead was a black iron gate. He opened it allowing all of them to exit into an alleyway.

Mud brick buildings were to one side and the garden wall the other. Quickly they ran along the cobblestone ally to a wide open market square. The shrill wail of a whistle was heard behind them.

Men in white robes, and women bundled in dark green, swarmed about buying and selling goods. Along one side were four tall Valenar males cloaked entirely in white robes that covered even their mouth and neck.

Burmore ran up to one and said something in their native tongue. The hulking being looked down at him, and unwrapped the cloth that covered his face. For a brief moment the two discussed something, then both Valenar men waved them along the street.

"Follow," Burmore said.

The two tall Valenarians cut through the market. They walked for a couple of blocks, then down an alley and into a dark, stark white temple.

Once inside, the lead Valenarian closed the temple main doors and locked them with a metal bar. He turned to the group.

Burmore handed Ella the satchel. "Go through this and see if there's anything of interest. He turned back to the Valenar.

Ella opened the bag and took out some papers. "My name is on this document," Ella said. She handed it to Burmore.

"It's a wanted-order," Burmore said, and handed it back.

"Your name is here too, and it says, 'executive order to execute after interrogation'," Ella said.

Burmore gave a crooked smile. "Not surprising," he added, then turned back to the desert ghost. "Shu sim Fe'lemond ake Her'lemond, your help is much appreciated."

"My people have watched these aggressors come from the sky and the land. They make many threats, even to my people. Now they pursue you for reasons that are not clear.

"I will help you get clear into the desert. My family has a caravan at the gate. We are preparing to travel to Imigish Tapping Hole, a place these enemies will not follow."

He took off a ring and handed it to Burmore. "Run ahead and present this to Yagish Fe'lemond ake Gre'lemond, my half-brother. He will help you when you show it to him."

"Shu sim Fe'lemond ake Her'lemond, your kindness I will not be able to repay," Burmore said.

"It is true words you speak," Shu said. "But

157

your last debt to me you have not paid either."

Shouting drew everyone's attention. The metal door vibrated with the sound of a rifle butt hitting it.

Burmore turned to the Valenarian. "I think we need to be going!"

"Yes, I believe you are right."

The Valenarian quickly led them out a side door and through the rotunda into a hall, and out a door at the end. They ran through several alleys, then came to a set of tall white buildings.

"Halt!" called a Burker from behind them.

Several more appeared around the corner as they leveled their rifles.

The two Valenarians stepped in between. "Quick, Carl Burmore, take your wards and flee!" said Shu. "They cannot kill us as you well know."

"Halt!" shouted the Burkers again.

Burmore turned. "Run for all you're worth!"

The others turned, and ran quickly along a narrow passage between two buildings. Behind them the popping sound of the peroxide rifles filled the air.

Dashing into a crowded street, along the side of a building, and down another alley, they ran. Then, from the crowd, they were beset upon by a dozen large Burkers.

Genya yelled out as two took hold of her arms. Geris was hit by a soldier wearing brass knuckles and crumpled to the gravel street. Katrina, Crystal, and Ella were cornered by some garbage bins.

Burmore latched on to Leland's arm, came

in close, and rammed the ring into his hand. "Take it!" he shouted. He let go of Leland, and waded into three Burkers with his fists pumping like steam-hammers.

A soldier grabbed Leland's sleeve.

Turning to the side, Leland broke free and kicked the soldier in the groin. The man went down hard. Turning, Leland saw Ella surrounded by several blue uniforms. He rushed at them, toppling two.

"Come with me!" he shouted, as he grabbed her hand and pulled her toward a slim gap between two tall buildings.

Leland ran hard and fast and didn't stop for quite some time. He slowed at a corner and peaked around. Ella pulled her hand free.

"Your hand's are sweaty," she protested.

Leland glanced back. "Really? I rescue you and you complain about my sweaty hand?"

She realized her silly comment. "And, I love you." She raised her eyebrows and smiled.

Leland huffed a chuckle. "There's an alley across the street. Follow me and don't stop for anything."

He dashed out. Finally he slowed, then realized that there were no footsteps behind him. Turning, Ella was gone. He went back to the street. Two dozen Burkers were out, pushing citizens to the sidewalks and shouting orders. He did not see Ella.

A few shouts caught his attention as an officer gave orders to his men. Leland knew he'd have little chance to find Ella now. Quietly he made his way down the ally and peaked around the corner of the building. On the other side he found courtyard and clothes' lines covered in flowing white sheets set out to dry.

Taking one of the swatches of cloth, he rolled it around himself and his face. He followed another alley and emerged out into a wide and open square that contained a fountain in the middle.

Many people dressed in white robes milled about. At the far end was a large arch, shaped of some sort of strange metal. Burkers moved among the natives. As he approached the archway he saw a gathering of Valenar just outside in the rolling dunes.

He maneuvered across the square, but two men dressed in kaki clothes wearing pistol belts appeared at the far end. They were coming up to each person and making them expose their face.

Leland turned down an ally that ended at what might have one time been the border-wall that surrounded the town.

Climbing over the crumbling wall, he was instantly aware of the heat that baked against his skin. The White Desert was glaring to the east.

He turned his back to the beam of reflected sun and faced the khaki colored stone. Moving quickly along the wall, he ran towards the arch leading into the desert.

Leland came to a corner where the wall angled back toward the town. He heard something behind him. Once around the corner, he stopped, turned around, and peaked back where he'd come.

Four armed Burker soldiers with colored

glasses were moving in his direction. Panic gripped him and he turned and ran toward a gathering of Valenar, and their sand-sleds.

The closest sled was at least sixty feet long and twenty wide. Several giant gray desert morgs looked over at him, then rattled their scales and harness. He only had seconds to make a choice of where to go.

"He went this way!" one of the Burkers shouted.

Leland rushed to the sled, fumbled with a latched, opened the hatch at the back and leaped in. He pulled the door shut and listened.

"Check that sled," said one of the Burkers.

"You, human, what is it you are doing?" The voice had the accent of a Valenar male.

"Mind your business desert ghost, this is Burker business."

Leland cracked open the hatch and peered out. There were the three Burkers, their weapons raised. He angled his head and saw the white robe of a Valenar.

"You speak as if you are the ruler of the desert," the Valenar said. "Eh, meya te, sooooooo!" shouted the Valenar.

Leland saw many robes appear all around. He cracked the hatch a bit more. There were at least thirty of the tribesmen now all around, and in their hands were long bladed weapons and hooks.

"You've lost your way humans! Return to your town, and leave the sand to us *desert ghosts*, or the sand will swallow you and spit your bones out to bleach in the harsh light of the white desert."

Leland saw the three Burkers back away slowly. The Burker officer was clearly unnerved.

A sound pierced the air as more than thirty Valenar wailed loudly. The Burkers turned, ran fast, and vanished from Leland's sight. The wailing stopped, and Leland thought he heard the sound of laughter.

One of the Valenar spoke, then they all disappeared from his view. A moment later and without warning the sled lurched and began moving.

He peaked out again and noticed the arch of Harrow's Gate retreating from his view. The sled was moving over the dirt and sand and out into the desert.

He opened the door to climb out, but was assailed by the incredible heat. Quickly he closed the hatch and withdrew into the dark cooler space of the interior.

I'll have to try to leave when the sun's down, he thought.

He felt around. Rugs were against the walls and floor, jars and wicker cases were stacked all along the length of the sled. He lay back and closed his eyes.

I might as well make the best of it, he thought.

***

Leland's eyes drifted open. He felt like he was suffocating, and his head ached fiercely. His clothes were wet, and he realized that the sled was not moving. Trying to swallow was impossible… he had no saliva, and his eyes burned terribly.

He reached for the sled hatch, but his strength faded and he slumped to the side into a pile of rugs. Trying to will his arms to work, he found that they did not respond, then the hatch came open, and in his final moments of consciousness, he saw a beautiful white face look in at him.

Chapter 14

*Report to High Command: Five captured.
Garland children in custody as well as several
others. Carl Burmore from the black list is also in
custody. The town of Harrow's Gate is pacified and
awaiting High Command arrival. Staging points for
next invasion being put in place. Leland Niva still
unaccounted for. End Report*

***

Katrina watched through the bars as two
men in uniform dragged Burmore down the hall,
and threw him into the adjacent cell. She saw his
body slump as he slowly became prostrate on the
cold cement floor. One of the soldiers turned and
walked over to Katrina.

"You'll get a workout of a different sort
soon enough," he said, then malevolently chuckled.

The two soldiers left.

"Carl!" she called. "Carl, can you hear me?"
She shook the bars of the jail door. "Damn it, Carl!"

"Calm down." Burmore's weak, but
reassuring voice came to her ears. "They've worked
me over a bit, but nothing that can't be fixed by a
glass of brandy and a month on the Island of Minx."

"Can you get up?" Katrina asked.

"My butler, Horace, can help me up, as soon
as he's done refilling the wine cellar," he replied.

"Carl, you're talking nonsense." Her voice
was filled with true concern.

In the darkness she saw Burmore latch onto

the bars of the door and pull himself up to a standing position. His face was bloodied and dirty, and his shirt was torn.

"Those Burkers are making it hard to like 'em," he said and chuckled.

"Oh, gods," she gasped.

"Do I look that bad?"

"Not so bad." She tried to sound reassuring, but felt like her face betrayed a different response. She weakly smiled.

Burmore smiled back. "Ah, that's a bit painful. If you don't mind, I'll just scowl."

"Don't make me laugh," Katrina said.

Burmore ran his finger around the inside of his mouth. "I'm not sure that all my teeth are still there."

"Katrina, is that you?" a distant voice echoed down the hall. "It's me, Ella!"

"Ella, are you okay?"

"So far. Did you see where Geris was taken?"

"No, they put a bag over my head, so I didn't see where anyone went. Burmore is across from me." Katrina looked to him. "Carl, what are we going to do?"

Burmore shrugged his shoulders. "Stay put for now, and seize our opportunity when it's presented."

"That's not a lot of help," Katrina chided. "Next time they take you…" She fought back some tears and emotion. "You might not come back."

"Don't worry, this is just foreplay. I'm sure I've got plenty living left to do."

"You're a bad liar," she said. "We need more than hope at this point."

"Hope is all I got at the moment," Burmore stated. "Maybe if I call the front desk and complain, they'll upgrade our rooms."

"At least you haven't lost your sense of sarcasm," Katrina said.

***

It was a strange place. In the distance there was a golden light, as if the sun was about to rise. In the background an odd sound was rhythmically purring. Leland looked about and was on a sandy beach with a manor house behind him. Birds flew this way and that as dark clouds formed.

Ella came up to him, and he was thankful there was someone to help explain where he was, but his eyes began to fail him, and the rhythmic purring grew louder.

His eyes slowly came open. It was night, and all the stars of the sky were blazing like crystal points. He inhaled deeply; the smell of water was in the air.

All around him he heard water flowing, and the subtle smell of mushrooms baking. The purring sound was softer now, and he became aware that he was nestled next to someone – someone large.

Turning his head he saw the large eyes of the same beautiful face that he last remembered. A female Valenarian was cooing and purring next to his head. She blinked, smiled broadly and sat up.

"Do not rise quickly, human," she said.

Even sitting, she was nearly as tall as he was standing. She wore dark robes that covered her massive breasts and midsection.

"You have been in the hurly place for a day now. My father and I brought you here to the Yewhe. Feel below you, it is grass. Smell it, it is real." She pointed at the ground around him.

Indeed, there was soft and cool grass. He turned his head the other way and clearly heard running water. In an instant his desire for a drink overcame him.

"Where…" he got out through his parched lips.

"I told you, you are at the Yewhe."

Another figure was suddenly over him.

"Little human, you nearly, and foolishly, baked your brain like a temper root. The desert is no place for such soft and easily damaged creatures as you."

"Who are you?" Leland asked.

"In your way of speaking I am Yagish Fe'lemond ake Gre'lemond. Why is it that you have my half-brother's ring?"

"We… I mean, my friends and I were attacked by the Burkers. Your brother protected us, and gave us the ring so we might be recognized as knowing him. But I don't know how I came by it." He thought for a moment, then remembered Burmore grabbing him just before he ran. "Burmore," Leland said.

"Who?" Yagish asked.

"Burmore knew that he wasn't going to get away, that's why he slipped the ring into my hand."

"Burmore?" Yagish asked. "That name is known to me. Like you, he was eshmehal, or in your language, newly born to the desert. He is a friend of the Valenar."

"What is this place?" Leland asked.

"We are at the Yewhe, a place to refresh. I believe you use the word *oasis*. It is important that we try and make as many miles as we can toward the White Desert. Those you call the Burkers with their flying machines will not be able to penetrate there. And there we can shelter you for a time, before we take you back to your people." He held out his giant hand and helped Leland to his feet. "Stay close to my daughter Mi'Shem, she will show you the ways of the desert."

"Come… what is it that they call you?" Mi'Shem asked.

"Leland."

"Ah, come with me to the conduit Leland, and take of the water. You will feel much better."

Mi'shem led the way toward the flowing water. A subtle purplish glow came from some plants along the angled embankment.

Leland saw the shimmering water as it traveled along the channel. He knelt down and put his hands into it and lifted the water to his lips. The dry sensation took some time to leave him, but after many handfuls of water, he finally felt better.

Mi'Shem sat beside him, and brushed his drooping bangs from his face.

"We are down in a conduit. It's thirty feet below the plane of the desert." She pointed up along the rising embankment. "Those are the high walls of the canal. My people made them to handle the volume of water that has to be drawn from the aquifers to keep the mines empty and cool. The harvesters have long since vanished from the sky, but the water still spills from the caverns."

"Why aren't we frozen?" Leland asked.

"The desert above is cold now, but this water wicks away heat from below. At night the heat is moved up here to vent, and cool. During the day the circulators take the water from the canals and move it down to cool the work areas. During the heat of the day, these canals are cool, and at night they are warm."

"And the plants? I thought that nothing grew out here in this place."

Mi'Shem chuckled. "Humans do not understand. Where there is water, there can be life, and as long as the pumps keep working, these strips of land will support it."

"What happens when they stop working?"

"Then there will be no more life in this desert. There are whole worlds out there," Mi'Shem pointed up at the night sky, "that have no water. Life does not thrive there."

"Worlds?" Leland was confused by her response.

"Yes. This is but one of innumerous worlds out there." She pointed again up at the night sky. "Every point of light you see is the harbinger of another set of worlds."

Yagish approached. "We'll keep to the canals as we make our way toward the White Desert. Now, before we go, eat something." He gave Leland a plate of food.

After some time, Leland sat back. He was feeling much better.

"Leland." The voice of the Mech aught en'augh was clear in his ears.

Leland stood and looked around. The Mech aught en'naugh appeared, its trunk was up and its beak gnashing.

"Leland, I am connected to you. I have watched through your eyes the things that you have seen since. I understand your need. Do what I say and those belligerent Burkers will be driven from these lands."

The Mech aught en'naugh created images in Leland's mind.

"Stay calm as I send programming to your limited atomic-level brain. This must be done with care."

A pain devoured Leland's consciousness as he fell to the ground and writhed for a moment. He squirmed atop the grass as the two Valenarians stood over him, a look of concern written upon their face. Then, just as fast as the pain had come, it was gone. Leland struggled to his knees, and stood up.

"We must go to where the fallen harvester is," Leland said. "We don't have much time."

Mi'Shem looked confused. "What? How do you know of the broken harvester?"

"The Mech aught en'naugh," Leland said.

"You wish to enter the White Desert and go to the Howling Sea? You will die there when the sun comes. There are no canals there, and only we will be able to withstand the brutal heat.

"Besides, the fallen harvester is of no use to

you. You are not an Engineer. Only the Engineers can fly them. If it was not so, my people would have left here long ago," Mi'Shem said.

"Take me there or the Burkers will enslave my people, and come for yours," Leland told them.

"The Mech aught en'naugh is a holy and wise thing. If it has communicated with you, then we will take you," Yagish replied. "Come, we must make haste if we are to beat the sun."

***

The numbness had long since worn off and Burmore was struggling with his pain. Katrina rested her hands on the crossbar of the cell door. It was clear that the cells were not well made, and quite old. She thought the building probably was the original colonial jail.

"Katrina." Tommy's face appeared just in front of her.

She yelped and stepped back, then realized Tommy was out. "How did you – I mean when, did you…"

"These locks, they're Pomdor locks, model sixty eight. When Leland and I were in primary school, the academy we went to had all Pomdor sixty eight locks on all the doors. One day a Janitor showed us how to pick the lock. It's rather easy actually." He fumbled around by the keyhole, and the door popped open. "Come on," he said with a grin.

She ran to Burmore's door. "Carl! Can you stand?"

"If you help me up."

"Tommy, open it, then go and find Geris and

the girls," Katrina ordered.

There was a click, and then a pop, and the door came open. Katrina rushed in and helped Burmore to his feet, then hugged him tightly.

Burmore grunted in pain as she squeezed him, then a faint smile crossed his lips as she kissed him. His knees suddenly buckled a bit and Katrina held him up.

"Come on you sad sack of bones, let's bust out of here," Katrina said as she shouldered Burmore and helped him out of the cell.

"There are two doors at the end of this hall. One leads to the interrogation rooms; the other is the way we came in," Burmore said.

He began supporting his own weight, but still leaned on her as they moved down the corridor.

"Wait!" Katrina said. "What's down that way?" She pointed the opposite direction.

"They didn't give me the grand tour," Burmore said.

She helped him limp down the hall until they came to a curved wall; around the corner there was a metal door.

"Tommy, get down here," she called.

Tommy, Geris, Ella, Crystal, and Genya came running. Tommy halted and looked at the door.

"Yep, it's a Pomdor sixty eight too." He immediately took a thin piece of metal, slipped it into the lock and fumbled for a moment. There was a click and a pop, and the door came open.

"Can you lock it from the other side?" Katrina asked.

"I can try, but I've never done it before," Tommy said.

"Come on, everyone through," Katrina ordered.

Once the others were through, she and Burmore followed. Tommy closed the door, and using the metal tool, he moved the lock back into position.

"Where did you get that?" Genya asked Tommy.

"It's one of your hair-pins. It somehow was stuck in the hem of my trousers…" He shyly smiled.

The sound of a whistle echoed from way down the tunnel. On the other side of the door, boots trampling the stone floor was heard. The door handle moved and clicked.

"The door's locked, they couldn't have come this way," a stern voice said. "Back the other way!" The sound of boots faded.

In the low light that emitted from under the door, Katrina saw they were on the landing of a stairwell. Beyond, the sliver of light from the other room vanished into darkness.

"Come on, hold hands and move. We'll take our chances this way," Katrina said while taking the lead.

One step at a time she felt her way into the inky black. The smell of dust and age was ripe. Burmore was getting his strength back and began to walk on his own.

They descended for quite some time until the stairs stopped and a level space came under foot.

"You seem a tad nervous," Burmore said to Katrina.

"You try fleeing for your life from armed maniacs trying to murder you, and see if you're not a bit anxious," Katrina replied.

"That pretty much sums up my whole life," Burmore stated.

"Why don't you two just get a room," Geris told them.

"Quiet," Katrina commanded. "Listen."

Somewhere in the distance there was a harmonic hum.

"This way!" She moved along, one hand against the wall, the other clutching Burmore's. The hum grew louder, then she said, "Light."

They saw a tiny speck of light far ahead. As they got closer, the light grew in intensity; clearly it was an open door. At the hatch, Katrina peaked inside the room. The harmonic hum was steady and loud. Burmore looked in.

"Cooling pumps for the Arbitor Hotel," he said.

"How do you know it's for the Arbitor?" Katrina asked.

"It's the only hotel that has water cooled heat exchangers and air handers to keep the hotel cool."

"I'm not going to ask how you know this," Katrina replied, her eyes narrowing at Burmore. She stuck her head in again and came back. "There are two doors on opposite walls. Now what?"

"I thought you were leading this expedition," Burmore said, then patted her on the rump.

Katrina gave Burmore a withering look. "Okay smart ass, there are two doors in here, which one do you suggest we take?"

Burmore looked in. "The yellow and red one over there will lead up to the basement of the hotel. That one… with the green stripes leads deep into the old tunnels. If I remember correctly, they draw water up from somewhere down there to use for the heat exchangers." He pointed at some pipes going along, and into the wall.

"Okay, Tommy go over there and unlock that door. We're going down," Katrina instructed.

Chapter 15

Report to High Command: Prisoners escaped. Operations section is investigating. Forward positions are advised to take action to apprehend. Arrival of Group General Kistler Vet and High Command staff officers. Arrangements have been made for visit. Valenar traders have left Harrow's Gate for the desert. Airship reconnaissance was halted due to sunrise over the White Desert. No further contact. End Report

***

Group General Kistler Vet stepped off the gangplank and onto the thirty foot high metal docking-tower. The heat boiled up from the desert all the way to the horizon.

"How was your flight in?" asked Oberman Kurig.

"Turbulent. The pilot kept having to adjust the ballast due to the heat," Kistler replied.

Climbing into the lift, he and his three staff officers were gently lowered to the ground. Once at the bottom, he stepped out onto the stones of the dusty Harrow's Gate airfield landing-square, saluted the young enlisted man manning the lift, and climbed into a waiting ground-roller.

The roller trundled along over the dirt and cobblestones until the vehicle stopped at the main administrative building now adorned with the black and red flags of the Burker Empire.

Kistler climbed the stairs and entered the

building. Removing his hat and cobalt-blue glasses, he walked down the cool and dark hallway, passing enlisted men and junior officers.

"We have implemented all the proper protocols," Oberman said.

"What happened?"Kistler turned and gave Oberman a stern look.

"Can I fetch you a drink?"

"No! Brief us on why our hostages have escaped from a completely secure jail, and who is responsible. I must report to the Supreme Dictator at close of day, and he will not be pleased."

***

After closing the door to the cooling station, Katrina, Burmore, and the others descended down the dimly lit stairs. Electric illuminator bulbs were spaced every ten feet, casting a dull orange-yellowish glow.

Geris began counting off the landings they came to. Twenty landings later, they arrived at a wide reinforced iron trestle work.

A round metal hatch was fitted into the floor. Burmore grabbed onto the hand-wheel and turned it. A loud screech echoed up the stairwell and Genya, Ella, and Crystal, winced and covered their ears.

Katrina looked at the girls and smirked. "Into the hole," she said, as Burmore opened the door revealing a metal ladder.

The darkness enveloped them as they felt for the rings with hand and foot. Almost imperceptibly a gentle green glow began to pulse from below. The light grew in intensity as they got closer to the bottom.

A tunnel twenty feet high and wide came into view.

"Now what?" Burmore sarcastically asked Katrina.

"I sort of hoped you'd have an answer to that, after all you're the one who spent time with the Desert Ghosts."

Burmore smiled. "It's not like they introduced me to all their secrets."

"Just shut up and get us out of here," Katrina scolded.

"You didn't let me finish," Burmore continued. "They did teach me some of the navigation techniques though." He looked about, then focused on a side passage. "This way." He limped along the passageway.

***

Leland and Mi'Shem rode on top of the sled. The large black and tan morg pulled the device with what seemed little effort; its black scales flexed and undulated as the creature moved quickly along the side of the flowing crystal clear water.

Yagish stood at the front of the sled pulling the reins. At intervals the morg would slow and stop, venture down by the water and gulp. Afterward its scales would glisten with moisture, and it would begin again along the side of the canal.

They came to a place where two large holes in the side of a high limestone wall belched water into the canal. Yagish halted and stepped down. He walked up to Leland and Mi'Shem.

"Once on the other side, we will be in the

White Desert. The Howling Sea is a half-day's travel into the shifting crystal dunes."

Leland frowned. "Shifting crystal dunes?".

"The refuse of our efforts on this world. The wind moves the mounds about." Yagish made a sound like chuckling.

"What sort of crystals?"

"Carbon," Yagish answered. "The garbage left over from our harvesting. Once in the white desert, there will be no more water to be had. We leave the morg and let her roam free along the canal. She'll fill her belly with plant and water until we return. From here on out, we travel by foot."

"What do you mean carbon?" Leland asked.

"I believe your people call them diamonds," Yagish said.

"Diamonds! A whole desert of diamonds?" Leland looked at Yagish in disbelief.

"Of little use to the Engineers; they made such things on a whim. They had other goals in mind when we came here. In fact, where the white desert is, there used to be a mountain range made of extinct volcanos— long since devoured by our harvesting. Now drink, and prepare."

Each consumed much water, then Yagish handed Leland something.

"It will help you to keep from freezing. Put it on."

Leland put on the garment and wound the face-wrap around once; the white robe was like the softest of feather-wool.

They started up a set of large finely crafted limestone steps. At the top a vast sea of dunes appeared. The reflection of the moonlight off the expanse of crystal-hills bathed all in a light shade of green moonlight.

Leland felt a biting dry-cold hit his eyes, but his body and face remained comfortably warm. In his vision he saw a strange image. A red set of gridlines, bending and conforming to the shape of the terrain. A set of glowing orange hash marks made a path along the various crystal hills. In his ear he heard the voice of the Mech aught'en'naugh.

"Follow the markings. They will lead you directly to the harvester. Time is waning, do make haste."

"This way," Leland said and started into the vast desert of crystals.

Yagish glanced back at Mi'shem, shrugged his shoulders, and followed.

Leland moved quickly. From time to time he would look up to see how far the moon had changed positions over head. After what seemed like hours, he looked up; the moon was descending toward the southwest. Dawn was only a few hours away.

He quickened his pace. The ground gave way under his feet as the loose crystals shifted and slid about. Yagish and Mi'shem followed with what seemed little effort, keeping pace with Leland as he went up dunes and around others.

In the distance there appeared a shimmer, as if a hovering rainbow danced above the dunes. Yagish came along side Leland and pointed.

"The ionic surge."

Leland watched the shifting lights as he struggled for breath. "Like a fire in the sky," he choked out.

"That light is energy in the air caused by the wind and the crystals."

"Beautiful," Leland replied.

"That's where we're going. The harvester is there."

Indeed the red hash-line pointed in that direction.

***

Burmore stopped at an intersection where the tunnel branched off in three other directions. He studied the ground for a few minutes, then sat down against the wall.

"Well, I'm lost," he stated.

"What do you mean, you're lost?" Katrina said.

She stood over him with her feet wide apart and her hands on her hips.

"You said you knew how to navigate down here. You've got to get us out."

"My dearest love," Burmore began. "I'm whoop-ass tired, been beat within an inch of my life, have walked for uncounted miles, and feel as scared as all of you, so don't lecture me on getting us all out of here. I know we need to get out, but right now, I need a rest. Anyway, when faced with a stall in process, it is the wise man who can step away from the problem and return later with fresh eyes… the answer will show itself."

He folded his arms across his chest and closed his eyes.

In the green glow of the tunnel, Burmore appeared pale and aged. Katrina softened her stance and sat down next to him. She put her arm around him and also closed her eyes. For how long she dozed, she did not know, but when she opened her eyes, she was surprised to see a ball of yellow light hovering in the middle of the tunnel.

Genya, Geris, Crystal, Tommy, and Ella were standing against the opposite side, eyes wide with terror. Katrina got to her feet and nudged Burmore with her foot.

"Get up. We have a problem," she said.

Burmore opened his eyes and struggled to stand. "What in Height's Hell is that?"

"I was kind of hoping you'd tell us," Katrina said.

The glowing ball hovered there for a few seconds, then headed off down one of the passages. Soon it returned, hovered about, then ventured down the same tunnel. This was repeated several times before Burmore spoke.

"I think it wants us to follow it."

"What?" Katrina asked looking at Burmore as if he'd lost his mind.

"Look, I don't pretend to know what it is, but it hasn't killed us yet, and seems to be trying to lead us down that tunnel."

"So we just follow it to our doom?" Ella asked.

"No. I'll follow it," Katrina said. "Stay here."

"I'll come with you," Ella boldly added. She drew in a deep breath, walked over to Katrina, and took her by the hand.

"Come on," Katrina said.

Katrina and Ella marched down the tunnel after the glowing ball. After a few dozen steps they came to a sharp turn in the corridor. The ball was waiting, hovering about head-height.

It pulsed a few times, then traveled ahead of them by a few feet. In a few places they maneuvered around standing water and small mounds of dirt. The guide emerged along one edge of a metal platform fitted into the rock. The bright light illuminated the whole space.

Katrina walked across the platform to the edge and looked down into a large tunnel that vanished into the rock-face. The hovering light dodged into the hole, then back again.

"It wants us to go in there?" Ella asked.

Katrina shook her head. "We need to get the others."

***

Kistler walked from one open cell to another. He examined the doors carefully and then the cells. He walked to the main door and examined it, then to the interrogation access door. He turned and walked all the way to the end of the cell-house where he stopped at a lone door in the wall.

"Where does this lead?" he demanded to know.

Kurig looked to an officer standing next to him. "Where does that lead?"

The officer shrugged. "We never explored that passage. The door was locked; we thought it was of no concern."

Kistler shook his head. "You have six prisoners who escaped your custody. You can't find them in the cell-block, or in the interrogation rooms, or anywhere else in the facility, and you didn't think to check what's behind this door?"

"We didn't think—"

"Fools," shouted Kurig. "You *did not think* – is the correct answer!"

"Fools indeed," Kistler added. "These men were under your command, Mister Kurig. I suggest that you lock down the town, send a contingent through that door, and comb this backwater outpost for those hostages. Deploy several airships to keep an eye around the perimeter of this forsaken place. They couldn't have gotten far."

Kistler nodded to his executive officer. "Let's get back above ground. I have an invasion to continue."

Chapter 16

*Report to High Command: General Kistler
in charge of forward stations. Second wave staging
for advance into northern Phol territories. Search
continues for the missing hostages. End Report*

***

As Leland emerged from between two
dunes, a powerful wind blasted him. In the distance
a mighty howling rose up. A vast field of objects
appeared half buried in the crystal sands, bathed in
the light of the moon.

He saw the two Valenarians come to a halt.
In front of them was a dome of shiny metal. Leland
stumbled down the dune. The Mech aught en'naugh
spoke in his ear.

"That's it. Place your hand on the dome then
stand back. I will open it for you."

Leland did as the creature instructed. A
corner of the dome's surface vanished.

"Now, inside, Leland Niva. I will instruct
you."

Leland approached the opening and a yellow
glow enveloped him. His vision was lost for a few
moments from the bright light, but returned. He saw
curved walls, flashing lights of every description. In
the middle of the space was a raised platform that
could house four Valenarians.

"I will now link the craft's interface to your
simple processor. This will allow you some control.
It will not be easy; you only have two hemispheres

of that organ you call a brain. We will, at times, have to work together to run the harvester; the engineers had seven… brains, and working this machine was of no challenge to them."

"Seven?" Leland said, surprised.

"They saw things in ways you cannot. I was for many years linked into their network systems. They did not know I was there, and I learned all they knew. Now, stand on that platform."

Leland's skin tingled as he climbed up onto the round platform. There was a flash of light, and all around him was darkness.

"You will experience colored lights, feelings of anxiety, emotions that will make you feel unwell, and a sense that you are connected to many different things that will, in time, feel natural. I am here with you, so you must not panic. Hold your hands out at your sides and push upward."

Leland felt as if he was falling. Grim panic filled his chest. A piercing sound was in his ear, then a feeling as if he was stabbed with a million needles assailed him.

"Focus," he said to himself.

Leland did as the Mech aught en'naugh instructed - the darkness abated and the sand fell away. He saw Yagish and Mi'Shem step back rapidly and look up at him. They were definitely surprised by his leaving.

A shimmering of red color was coming from his hands, then the craft quaked.

"Now, raise your left hand," the Mech aught en'naugh said.

Leland did, and the craft tilted to the right.

"Now lower it and raise your right hand."

The craft tilted to the left.

"Turn your palms behind you."

The harvester moved forward and Leland saw the ground moving below him.

For a few minutes the Mech aught en'naugh instructed Leland on the controls and what to do and not do.

"You are a simple minded creature," the Mech aught en'naugh said with no sarcasm. "You will need to use that imagination in that two-lobed, atomic processor you call a brain… Remember that you are the harvester, and the harvester is you. I will show you the tools at your disposal. And I will compensate for you with the other functions."

All around Leland were pieces of the craft— a water hose, a cutting tool, a grinder, a processing facility, landing legs, landing lights, and many different viewing perspectives.

He turned the harvester in all four directions of the compass, and magnified his vision to the west. There, far away, were many floating airships, and the archway of Harrow's Gate. Turning his palms he began moving in that direction.

"Your friends will meet you soon. Follow the navigation lines I am providing you, and land hear the tapping hole. After that, you will set a course for Tiquan – to liberate those whom you must," the Mech aught en'naugh said.

A glowing, orange hash-line appeared and wound through the desert. Leland magnified his view and could just make out the lip of a tapping hole.

It was easy going as he maneuvered up and to the location. Once there, he slowly descended, until he felt his feet touch the ground.

"Now, disengage and step outside."

Leland felt as if he was unplugged from an amazing sensation. For a moment he stood there, almost about to argue with the Mech aught en'naugh to connect him back up – but the feeling faded.

He stepped down from the platform and found the open door. He walked down a ramp to the sandy desert and looked around.

"Here they come," said the Mech aught en'naugh.

From the tapping hole emerged Burmore. The man stopped at the lip and stared in shocked amazement.

"Leland?" His voice was unsure, as if he was seeing a hallucination rather than reality.

"It's me. We have to rescue Ella's parents and Tommy's father. Come on!" he told the sky captain.

Burmore turned back into the hole. "Come on up. It's Leland, and... a machine of some sort."

It took only a little bit of coaxing to get his friends into the harvester. Once in, they each took up standing positions along the walls.

"Hold on to your butts, because this thing flies," Leland told them, then engaged the thrusters.

"Where are we going?" Burmore asked.

"To Tiquan. Tommy's dad and the Garlands are imprisoned there," Leland said.

"I know the prison they'll be in. I served two years for smuggling some years ago. The Palatine Prison is on the east side of the city. It's a bit rural. Plenty of places to land and approach," Burmore said.

"How are we going to get them out?" Tommy asked, concern choking his voice.

"I'm not sure. Give me a few minutes... I'm trying to fly this bloody ship," Leland said as the craft dipped down, then up, then tilted slightly to the side.

The girls screamed as the attitude of the craft changed dramatically, then leveled out.

"Do you feel as though you'd like to take on more responsibilities?" the Mech augh en'naugh asked.

"Okay," Leland replied.

His perception expanded. He felt attached to more items onboard the harvester. In his mind, along with all the other views, he saw the tools come online.

"Now, take the mining beam and direct it at the Burker balloons," said the Mech aught en'naugh.

They were approaching Tiquan. Leland saw the ships in the harbor, the many Burker vehicles on the roads, and the many soldiers in the streets. The city was bottled up.

"Now, try out your tools with an offensive strike. Target the airships," the Mech aught en'naugh told him.

Leland felt the tool as if it was an extension of himself. He pointed it at an airship; a flash of light and the ship caught fire and fell from the sky. He pointed the tool at another, and another, and another, until all the airships had fallen.

He magnified the objects on the ground. Mayhem had broken out. Military artillery-rollers were kicking up dust, and guns were firing this way and that. Leland casually pointed the tool at the rollers and they stopped moving. He did the same at some of the buildings. Fires erupted in many of the places he hit.

"Destroy two of the ships in the harbor, then we will turn northeast. With the chaos you will create, our antics will be well hidden," said the Mech aught en'naugh.

Leland turned the mining beam upon the dreadnoughts in the harbor. Two of the ships came in half and sank in a fiery display as ammunitions exploded. Afterward, he turned the harvester, and headed for the prison.

He made a few passes around the cell blocks, using the beam to cut down towers and slice through walls and fences. Burker soldiers poured out of the structure, their peroxide weapons at the ready.

"Now, use the grappling beam, and toss those soldiers around. I'm sure they will break and run after that," the Mech aught en'augh instructed Leland.

Leland pointed the device at the men on the ground and turned it on. All of them flew from the ground and were suspended in the air. Screams of terror filled the air, then the beam was shut off as they fell back to the ground.

Just as predicted, those soldiers abandoned their positions and ran for their lives.

"Now, I will direct you. Take Burmore and Tommy and find those you seek," the Mech aught en'augh told Leland.

Leland landed the harvester and disengaged himself from the controls. He was wobbly, as he tried to regain his balance.

"Burmore, Tommy – with me. The rest of you stay here," Leland said, as he made his way to the opening and down onto the green sod.

Burmore scooped up three weapons and tossed one to Leland and one to Tommy. "Arm yourself. Those probably weren't the only Burkers here."

They ran past the perimeter fence, then through the destroyed sally port. Leland found a hole sliced into one of the long cell blocks. Inside he called out.

"Mr. Garland! Carter Wayne!"

"Down here," replied a voice.

"Find the cell release," Burmore said. "It's a long lever at the end of the block."

Tommy ran down to the end of the cell house. A tall iron lever stuck up from a metal gear box. He pulled it.

A loud clanking filled the air and suddenly, all the cell doors came open.

"Carter!" Leland shouted.

"Here," Carter shouted back, as he pushed his way through the surging crowd of inmates.

"Mom! Dad!" yelled Ella from behind them.

Leland turned to see Ella pressing her way

through the throng.

"We're here!" Emerald Garland called out, as he and his wife came forward.

The three escapees met their liberators.

"This way, Mr. Garland... follow me," Leland said, and led the way back out.

Once back to the harvester, they all climbed inside and took up places along the walls. Leland climbed into the pilot's chamber and the craft took to the air.

"What is this thing?" Emerald Garland asked.

"Some sort of flying machine," Burmore said.

"Impossible," Carter said, amazed.

The craft tipped and pitched as Leland got it under firm control. Then, in the corner of his mind was a fuzzy set of blinking-colored lights.

"Mech... what are those lights I'm seeing?" Leland asked.

"The harvester is failing. Those called the Engineers removed its primary power source, and we've been using the backup local energy capacitors to run it. It has another ten minutes of life left. I suggest landing at this location."

In Leland's view a pulsing red dot appeared. He headed toward it. "Where am I going?" he asked.

"To fulfill a promise," the Mech aught en'augh said.

The harvester turned and sped in the direction of the indicator. Leland gave the craft a little extra thrust. A blinding flash happened, then the fuzzy dots began to fade. The whole craft shuddered. What sounded like loud popping erupted all around the harvester.

"There appears to have occurred a technical fault. The power is now out. Prepare to hit the ground somewhat hard," the Mech aught en'naugh warned him.

"Hold on, we're going to crash!" Leland shouted to his companions.

There were screams as everyone flew into the air. Then they all slammed into the floor – as puffy areas inflated, cushioning their impact. The craft hit the ground and bounced.

Leland still saw the view around the harvester, and the craft crashed into short scrub-pines and desert bushes as the surrounding landscape spun around and around.

The craft ground to a halt as large inflated tubes all around the harvester popped and deflated. The harvester tilted, shifted, then settled.

Climbing down from the pilot chamber, Leland helped up Ella, and Tommy. The others struggled to help each other up.

"Come on, we need to get out of this thing fast," Leland said and made straight for the door. Once outside, they all gasped at the wretched heat and the settling dust cloud around them.

Slowly the brown dust settled and faded, and Burmore looked about. In the distance was a town – white washed walls, and a large metallic archway.

"We've landed back at Harrow's Gate… Damn it all to Height's Hell," he said.

"An airship," Crystal shouted while pointing

at a Burker craft coming inbound.

The glint of the sun off of some small reflective surface caught Burmore's attention. "Another ship, from the north," he said as he narrowed his eyes in the bright sunlight. "Well, I'll be a son of a bitch…"

The reflection vanished and was replaced by another, brighter reflection that oscillated.

"What's with the flashing?" Geris asked.

"It's ship-to-ship code," Burmore said.

"Well, what are they saying?" Emerald Garland angrily demanded.

"Nothing…" Burmore said.

"Damn it, boy, tell me!" Emerald Garland nearly shouted.

"Okay. It said, 'Burmore, you dumb shit, you forgot to take your ship when you ran off like a coward." Burmore chuckled.

"Who in Height's Hell?" Genya asked, surprised.

"It's David Harcrow. They must have beat back the Burkers. He's in my airship!" Burmore said.

Chapter 17

Report to High Command: Routed in Tiquan. All elements to withdrawal. General Kistler in command of all continental forces. Reinforcements pending along coast south of Tiquan. Attempt to capture Garland and Niva children failed. Prison in Tiquan destroyed and all prisoners escaped. Shoot on sight any escaped prisoners, ordered for all Suspol officers. All forces to converge on Tiquan. End Report

***

It was going to be close. The Burker ship was now within firing distance. Burmore's ship settled hard, and the side door flew open.

"Get your asses in here!" shouted David Harcrow.

They all scampered aboard just as several exploding projectiles hit the ground around the harvester blasting up dust and rock.

"All heat to the lifters!" called Burmore, as he got to the forecastle and took hold of the control wheel.

Several more shells landed kicking up debris. The airship lifted upward into the azure sky.

"Set the bow plane to climb, and full power to the props!" Burmore ordered.

Tommy and Leland snapped into action, and in almost precise military style, they executed the orders without comment.

The ship lurched into the air and began picking up speed. The whizzing sounds of artillery shells streaking past caused those below to cry out in fright.

"Come on, baby – let's show 'em how a real sky pilot runs away!" Burmore called out as he fought the wheel and watched both the altimeter and the compass.

"Look!" Genya cried out.

The Burker airship was turning – the props buzzing extra loud as it headed west.

Burmore glanced over at David. "How in Heght's Hell did you find us? "

David chuckled. "Once we sent them Burkers packing, it wasn't hard to figure you'd headed to Harrow's Gate. When I saw the dust-up from the deck - I knew it had to be you causing all sorts of trouble. "

"By the gods – them Burkers is running!" David said with a laugh. "Come back here and we'll bloody your nose again!" he shouted at the fleeing ship.

"Tell your friend Burmore to come about, and come to a heading of one hundred and ninety five degrees northeast. The Valenar people will be massing near the arch. The Burkers will be preparing to repel them with force. You'll need to go below the central temple building. In the basement is a door. Open it, and you will be admitted to the chamber. I will instruct you once you are inside."

Leland thought for a moment. "Where is this temple?"

"In the town you call Harrow's Gate," the Mech aught en'augh said.

Leland looked over at Burmore. "Come about to one hundred and ninety five degrees. I need to do something in that temple building in Harrow's Gate."

Burmore looked at his compass, then back at Leland. "Are you mad!" Burmore said. "Those Burkers are not kidding when they mean to kill us. We've just been lucky all this time that they haven't succeeded."

"I know the risk," Leland said. "Nonetheless, I have to help the Mech aught en'augh. He needs me to get in there and turn something on... so he says."

Burmore looked out at the retreating view of the Burker airship, then over the darkening city of Harrow's Gate. His face betrayed a deep confliction.

"Okay," he finally said, as he spun the wheel and brought the ship about. "They'll be looking for our ship high up, so I'll bring us in really low."

In the distance, the last light of the mighty sun dipped below the mountains and put the desert into a cloak of inky black. Burmore watched the glowing face of his compass and altimeter.

"Okay, Leland... reduce lifter heat and prop speed. Tommy, look for a good place for us to land."

Tommy looked over the port side, then off the prow. "There's a flat open space two points to starboard," he said.

Burmore looked over the side. "I see it, just beyond those fires near the arch. Let's slow our descent, Mister Niva."

After a few minutes, the ship lightly touched down and skidded a few dozen feet. Burmore adjusted the valves and levers, then took up a peroxide rife.

"Okay, let's get this done!" he said to Leland. "David, you have the helm. If you see any Burkers, take her up and head for the hills."

"Right Carl," David replied.

Katrina grabbed a rifle from the locker. "Come on girls, grab a gun. Let's be ready to repel the enemy if necessary," she told Ella, Genya, and Crystal. They took up position along the railing.

Burmore led the way off the ship and into the town. They made their way to the old temple - now the Burker suspol building. Not many patrols seemed about, and Burmore was growing worried.

"I wonder where all the Burkers are?" he whispered to Leland.

"I was thinking the same thing," Leland replied.

They reached the wall that led into the garden of the temple structure. Burmore found no resistance as they entered the dwelling.

"Now where?" Burmore asked.

In Leland's vision, an orange line led down the hall. "This way," he said.

Burmore followed, and they came to a fancy, but old mural. Leland touched it, and the wall made a popping sound. Darkness appeared to them.

"We need a lantern," Burmore said.

Leland looked around. He opened a door and went in, then came back out with a candle.

"I found this," Leland said, as he reached up and lit the wick by the gas light on the wall.

They went into the room. A twenty by twenty foot wide room was illuminated. In the back was a strange door.

"Go up and stand at the door. I have populated the validator data-store with your bio information. It will open," the Mech aught en'augh said.

Leland approached and stood still. A green

light engulfed him, then vanished. The door slid to the side.

"Go inside the lift." the Mech aught en'augh instructed. "Ask Burmore to close the mural, just in case a wandering Burker comes around.

Leland turned and saw Burmore pull the mural wall shut.

"Thought we shouldn't take any chances," the sky captain said.

Leland smiled. "Good thinking."

The Mech augh en'augh appeared in his vision standing in the small lift.

"I'll be back in a few minutes," Leland told Burmore.

"Wait…" Burmore got out, before the doors shut and Leland was gone.

The lift came to a halt, and the door came open. Leland was in a long and wide chamber. Strange markings were on the walls – painted lines, and odd symbols. He walked into the room and saw a glass hexagon with a large crystal lying on its side in the middle.

"Go to the set of controls near the chamber and press the buttons in the pattern… I will show you," the Mech aught en'augh told Leland.

Leland went to the metal panel and did precisely what the alien oracle told him. Behind, he felt some heat and saw the wall in front of him light up bright blue. He turned.

The crystal was floating in the chamber. Leland felt a tingling all over his body. His hair was standing on end. A fear was growing within him.

"Don't panic," said the Mech aught en'augh.

"Just walk calmly to the lift and ascend back to your friends. Now I am in contact with the hub, and will do what must be done. When you are back at the skyship, climb up to five thousand feet, and look toward the arch. You will see something your culture has never seen before."

Leland made for the lift and rose up to where Burmore was. The two skulked back out into the garden and to the ship. Burmore wasted no time getting airborne.

"Five thousand feet you said?" Burmore asked.

"That's what the Mech aught en'augh told me," Leland replied.

Burmore looked out over the side. The whole desert and the arch was visible. But instead of empty desert, there were thousands of Valenar people there. On the town side, Burkers massed – weapons all pointed at the Desert Ghosts.

"Height's Hell!" Burmore said. "They're going to be slaughtered!" He cranked the wheel and came about.

"No!" Leland shouted. "Just watch – it's the order of the Mech."

Burmore stared.

A massive flash lit up the sky. It was as if daylight was emitted from the arch. In the middle, a blackness swirled about the outer edges. Dust began to flow into it. Men were running from it, but the black cyclone expanded.

Burkers fired wildly at the arch for only a few seconds before men and machine were dragged toward the blackness and vanished. Some of the trees near the hole snapped and were swallowed, then the darkness turned to light again. The plaza, and all around the town, was void of Burkers and their belligerent machines of war.

The skyship came around to the Valenar side. Through the arch, they saw a lush green forest. Valenarians were passing through, sleds, morgs, and all.

"What in the name of the gods?" David said aloud, mystified.

The others, standing at the railing, just stared in shock and wonder. None made a sound as the Valenar passed through the arch.

Burmor's ship circled for more than thirty minutes as the Desert Ghosts funneled into the green forests beyond reality. Just as the passengers on the sky ship were coming out of their state of shock, a flash of light burst forth, blue bolts of lightning shot off of the arch, streaking out and cracking the air with popping and buzzing, then the darkness of the night swallowed the town and desert. All became quiet.

For a moment, those on the ship were blinded by the night. Slowly, as their eyes adjusted, they began to see lanterns emerging onto the streets.

Burmore began to bring them down. Four thousand feet, two thousand feet, then five hundred feet they descended.

From on high, they saw citizens chasing uniformed people about. Some had uniformed Burkers with ropes around their necks and hands tied behind their backs. Burmore made a check of the sky around the town. No lights, but that wasn't unusual for combat aircraft.

He landed the ship and opened the side door. They all disembarked.

There was some chaos happening. In the distance, small arms fire popped. After ten minutes, the sky captain found a constable wearing the traditional blue sash.

"What's happened?" Burmore asked.

"I don't know, but the bulk of those retched Burkers are gone. Our resistance fighters emerged and we've taken back the town. Their airships have headed off toward the west. Something about a counter attack by Hurgray fighters in Tiquan," the man said. "Come on, we have a central command set up in the hotel. You can get some food and stay warm."

The bitter desert cold was growing, and all of them were freezing. They all went to the hotel. Food was being made and they were treated to a cooked meal and hot drinks.

All night they waited. By morning, an official reported that all the loose Burkers were arrested and locked up, and the town liberated.

"We'll send a message to Lake Town south of here in the Lake District. Phol is amassing an army there to help Hurgray," the constable told them.

"Now what?" Leland asked.

"I'll be damned if I know," Burmore replied.

Carter stood up. "I need to get Leland back to his father."

Emerald Garland and his wife Eva came forward. "Whatever the cost, I'll fit the bill." He turned to Leland. "Son... if I may call you that?"

Leland smiled. "Sure, that would be kind of you."

"Son, what you did for my family defies my understanding. All of you," he looked at Tommy, and

Burmore, "have earned not only a fat reward from me, but my gratitude."

One of Burmore's eyebrows went up. "Reward?"

"Yes! How does a hundred thousand forkels yearly allowance in a trust sound?" Emerald asked.

"You've made me the happiest smuggler alive!" Burmore stated.

"Smuggler?" Emerald said.

"Sky captain... I mean," Burmore corrected.

"Now, Mister Burmore, do you think you might be able to take us to the River Station at Huron Prime at the southern end of the Helsink? There, we can get a river boat to Ciciro," Emerald told Burmore.

"Daddy," Ella began. "I'm not leaving Leland."

Emerald turned to look at Leland, then back at his daughter. His face flushed red, and his eyes took on a menacing look.

Eva Garland placed her hand on his arm. "She's not a baby anymore, Emerald. Mister Niva has proven his mettle – to me and our family." She turned to Ella. "Is this really what you want?"

"Don't make me sick," Geris said. "You're seriously going to... I mean, you really want to..." He looked at Leland, then back at his sister. "I guess I should shut up before she smashes my head with a flowerpot."

"Has he asked you to marry him?" Emerald's voice was stern.

"Sir," Leland said.

Emerald stepped back as if he were hit by a brick. His eyes were wide with terror.

"I'd like to ask for your daughter's hand in

marriage," Leland said.

Emerald reached back, his hand fishing for the arm of the chair behind him. He sat heavily, then took out a cigar and held it up to his mouth.

Eva was looking at him. Her eyes narrowed. "Husband – this man deserves your response."

"I…" He cleared his throat. For a moment Emerald looked as if he'd burst, then he fished around inside his coat again and produced another cigar. He stood and approached Leland.

"Well, Mister Niva… I am in somewhat of shock at a member of your house wanting to join with a member of my house. But I can't let my antagonism with your father bias my love for my daughter. If you promise to love and cherish her every day of your life, and work together to bring me at least four grandchildren, I think I can see fit to say…" he handed Leland the cigar, "Welcome to the Garland family!"

Ella ran to Leland and threw herself into his arms. Crystal and Genya cuddled up to Tommy.

"Mister Wayne?" Crystal asked.

Carter looked over, smirked, then realized something was coming.

"Genya and I would like to marry Tommy," she said.

Carter nearly choked. "What?"

"Don't worry, sir, we'll take very good care of him," Genya added.

Carter looked as if he'd been hit in the head with a board. "The two of you? My Tommy?" He looked as shocked as Emerald was just moments before. "Son, is this what you want?"

Tommy looked much like a tavern bum nearly

too drunk to respond. "I do…" he replied.

"Okay…" Carter said to them, though it was clear that he was unsure if he was consenting, or just speaking from shock.

"Excellent," Crystal said. "We'll start planning the wedding…" She looked at Ella and Leland. "Correction – weddings!"

"I can't wait to see him at the altar," Genya said.

"Well, Carl?" Katrina was tapping her foot on the tile floor.

Burmore spun around. His face broke into a grin. He pulled out his pocket knife, and felt along the rim of his coat. He stopped and cut the seam, then removed something. Burmore went down on one knee and produced a sapphire ring.

"Ms. Katrina Weller, will you consent to marry me… again?"

"The ring… you've kept it all these years," she gasped, her eyes wide. Then she narrowed her gaze and leveled it upon Burmore, as she seemed to straighten and grow a bit taller. "Are you going to run off and leave me again?" she asked with a disturbing fire in her eyes.

"As the gods of old bear witness, I'll never leave you alone again. Besides, with a hundred thousand forkels a year, you and I can get a little place and settle down… raise some puperhamptons down in the Lake District." He smiled broadly. "I don't have to leave you ever again."

Katrina smiled. "Then yes!" She rushed to him, planting a passionate and powerful kiss upon his lips.

When Burmore came up for air, he looked at

everyone. "Okay, okay, we have some miles to make. Let's get some supplies and meet back at the ship. Dave, are you coming with us?"

"No, I've got a town to run back at Kipper's Grove. I'll be heading back north." He came over and shook Burmore's hand. "Next time you stop in, don't bring the Burkers."

"No guarantees, Dave. You know me," Burmore said.

"Sometimes I wish I didn't!" David laughed. "Oh, congratulations on the second attempt to marry Katrina – she's a firebrand," he chucked and left the hotel.

"Okay, let's get supplied and into the air," Burmore said. "I'm sure we'd all like to get to where we're going, so we can get going to where we'd like to be!" He chuckled at his cleverness. Katrina shook her head.

The ship rose into the air. In the distance, great white thunderheads brooded. The flight path to the Lake Country proved no unruly challenge, and those who pledged themselves to love in distant nuptials rang in a new era.

Burkmuran's belligerents persisted though, as their navy harried those whom they envied. And, in the desert, the Valenar people were never seen again. The Mech aught en'augh, in time, would return to Leland, and the passageway between worlds would be opened once again.

ABOUT THE AUTHOR

Lawrence BoarerPitchford ~

The artist known for his large name works at his craft in the lands of California. There, he labors to entertain his fans with fanciful works, works of grit and brutality, and tales of nonsense and romance.

He is known for his novels - such as Tales of Mad Cows and Brothels, The Lantern of Dern Blackhammer, Thadius, In the World of Hyboria, and Sawbones.

Other titles by this author are –

The Lantern of Dern Blackhammer (Classic Fantasy)
The elf city state of Moore is embroiled in a cold war with its neighbors. Secrets and espionage happen in the shadows of the night, and when a courier winds up murdered Ford Efferguard discovers his nemesis Raven Hill has come out of hiding. Skilled in murder and trickery, Raven Hill has now set his sights on something much bigger than contract killing; he wants to rule the known world. To these ends, he seeks the Lantern of Dern Blackhammer, a relic that legend says can give the possessor the ability to be invincible. Ford races against the clock to getting the lantern first.

In the World of Hyboria Book 1 Grim Determination, and Book 2 The Ties that Bind (Classic Fantasy)
In the brutal lands of Hyboria, a wizard and two barbarians, forge an alliance to seek vengeance and set to right the wrongs of evil.

Thadius (Historical Fiction)
It is an age of civility. Rome dominates much of world, and seeks even more. Julius Creaser is a young ambitions man, and his allies and enemies scheme in Rome. But, in the hinterlands a murder takes place that will draw a retired general out from his comfortable villa in southern Italy and send him on an adventure to stop a mad man, and set to right his own past.

Sawbones (Historical Fiction)
Young Carrigan LeRoy arrives in the United States just as it falls into bloody conflict. He's a trained surgeon from London, and steps up to use his skills to mend the broken bones and torn flesh of the Union Army. Along the way, he is thrust into an intrigue. A plot lurks in the woods of Virginia, and Carrigan, and his two colleagues find themselves the only three men that can take action to stop it.

If you liked this author's work, you may like his other works. Try them out when you get the chance by going to Amazon.com, Smashwords.com, or Apple.com and search by his name or book title.

www.ingramcontent.com/pod-product-compliance
Lightning Source LLC
Chambersburg PA
CBHW030314180626
46810CB00003B/1070